A FOREST DARK

J.A. WALDIN

— WALDIN BOOKS —
Toronto, Canada

WALDIN BOOKS
Toronto, Canada
JAWALDIN.COM

FIRST EDITION

ISBN: 978-0-9920893-1-3

To:

Dad & Mom

&

Those that suffer —

Might this be a light on dark days

Midway upon the journey of our life
I found myself within a forest dark,
For the straightforward pathway had been lost.

Ah me! how hard a thing it is to say
What was this forest savage, rough, and stern,
Which in the very thought renews the fear.

So bitter is it, death is little more;
But of the good to treat, which there I found,
Speak will I of the other things I saw there.

I cannot well repeat how there I entered,
So full was I of slumber at the moment ...

[... and Virgilius said:]

Therefore I think and judge it for thy best
Thou follow me, and I will be thy guide.

— Dante Alighieri, *Inferno*

If you are going through hell, keep going.

— Winston Churchill

A FOREST DARK

[PROLOGUE]

Time is but the stream I go a-fishing in. I drink at it; but while I drink I see the sandy bottom and detect how shallow it is. Its thin current slides away, but eternity remains. I would drink deeper; fish in the sky, whose bottom is pebbly with stars.

— Henry David Thoreau

"We are not our thoughts, we are not our emotions," the instructor said, looking round to see what weight his words held. He sat at the head of the circle. A group of people, young and old, surrounded him: a young woman from New York who had suffered from anxiety ever since the 9/11 attacks; an elderly East Indian woman, her face just beginning to show her age; a marketing consultant; a painter; and Philip, a young man, tall, who would be considered handsome if he took the time to shave and to trim his unruly hair. His beard covered his cheekbones and his hair obscured his blue eyes.

These and eleven others sat in the circle. Some, like Philip, cast their eyes down, occasionally stealing a glance at the instructor. Others wrung their hands and exuded a nervous energy that wafted around the conference room.

That conference room Philip Hyde would remember, with its burnt-orange industrial carpeting and high windows, long after this day. More than anything else, Philip would remember those windows, which allowed light to cascade into the room and granted a view of the low brownstone buildings and the heavily treed campus of the University of Toronto.

It was fall, and the leaves had begun their inebriating colour exhibition. The conference room was in a back office area of the Centre for Addiction and Mental Health (or CAMH, as it is widely known in Toronto), on the fifth floor. Philip was glad for this, for being in the back of the building; they entered through trees, across a small parkette, and down quiet and empty hallways. He was glad for this, as the hospital proper was a bit creepy. The skyward-sweeping façade, all hard edges and unfinished concrete, made it look more like Stasi headquarters than a place of healing.

Philip and his colleagues were in a new and unusual program: Mindfulness-Based Cognitive Therapy for Depression, or MBCT.

"We are never told this in school, we are never asked to discuss it, we never talk about it. But this does not change this irrefutable fact of human beings ..." continued the instructor.

And?! thought Philip. He was here for depression, and he had it bad. Sometimes when asked to describe it he would say it's like someone following you around from day to night with a loaded gun pointed at your head. Or, if he was talking to someone nautically inclined like himself, he would say it was like riding a sailboat in a hurricane, in the pitch of night, in waves as large as apartment buildings, and all the chatter on the radio is about knitting. Given that, he wondered, so motherfucking what if we're not our thoughts or emotions?

"These things only matter experientially. I could sit here and attempt to explain their importance till I'm blue in the face, but today we're going to experience it. Or at the very least, we're going to attempt to give you the tools to experience it."

Philip sat at the edge of his chair, like all the others, in preparation for meditation, but he, unlike the others, ground the edge of his chair with white knuckles. At times the pain was unbearable.

When he had entered the program, he had been given a questionnaire. He'd sat in a cramped office, between stacks of files and books. An Indian woman, a nurse, had proctored the questionnaire, dressed in an Indo-classical pantsuit, and a brightly coloured one at that. The bright green and red seemed to say, "I am a woman, and that is something to celebrate. You know what I mean." Her liquid brown eyes had a soft look to them. She had given him the questionnaire about his health — how much do you sleep, how much do you eat, and so on — but question 19 had stopped him cold. "On a scale of 1 to 10, 1 being never and 10 being all the time, how much do you think about death, self-harm, or suicide?" He had studiously left that question blank.

He slipped the questionnaire back to the woman after he finished. She received it with a smile and began to mark off each answer and record them in a file.

"You've left question 19 blank," she said, passing the form back to Philip. "We need answers for all the questions." Philip nodded and took the form, noting that her tone was bizarrely neutral. Did she understand the weight of the question? He looked at the form and circled 10. He tried in vain to stifle a deep sigh as he passed the form back. She looked down at the form and back at him. A spark of compassion filled her brown eyes.

He was here for help, but at times the intensity of his pain became worse instead. Today his mind shrieked and rebelled. He knew he was preparing to go into his mind. He was young, he was strong, he knew this, but the pain ...

Courage, he said to himself, in the French way.

"... It's a bit like that old joke — I always thought the brain was the most important organ in the body until I realized what was telling me that," continued the instructor, who smiled despite the fact that he got no response from the group. Philip shook his head imperceptibly and looked the man over. He wore a pressed blue dress shirt tucked severely into his khaki pants, was cleanly shaven, and spoke from the edge of his chair, his posture military straight.

Doesn't look much like a meditation teacher, Philip thought, and not for the first time.

"Close your eyes," the instructor said.

They did so. Philip sat in the darkness, his thoughts and emotions swirling behind his eyelids.

"Breathe in ... and breathe out ... Feel your breath."

Philip did this. The room fell silent and all he could hear was the sound of his own breath in his ears. He felt his breath expand in his chest. He sought the turning point, as they had been taught in previous weeks, the point where in-breath turned to out-breath. Then, like a shot ringing out into the clear blue sky, his mind whirled away. What am I doing here? ... What is this? ... I just want to feel better ... He noticed this. He gave himself points for it, as he sought to bring his attention back to his breathing.

"If you notice that your attention is no longer on your breath, bring it firmly, kindly, back to the feeling of your breath. Congratulate yourself for bringing your mind into the present moment," the instructor said into the silence of the room. A sense of calmness descended on that room, with no sound but the rasping of sixteen breaths.

Philip breathed. And again ...

"Note where your mind goes, when your attention leaves your breath, and then simply return your attention, kindly and gently, to your breathing."

Why in the name of all that is holy am I doing this? thought Philip, but he caught that thought and returned to the feeling of the air running down his throat. That's a pleasant feeling, he thought, and he caught that one too.

He breathed.

"Now we're going to turn our attention to our thinking. We are going to look at the content of our thoughts. Try to think of your thoughts as images moving across a movie screen or as clouds moving through the sky. Watch them

appear in your consciousness. Note the emotional weight they may or may not have. Then watch them disappear from your consciousness."

Philip breathed.

"If you feel yourself getting caught in the content of the thinking, this is fine. Note this and return to your breathing."

A silence filled the room, an energy. It was as though stone walls had been erected around their circle. Ancient stones, black and mossy, and the air pressure inside these walls sank.

Philip attempted to do as instructed, to watch his thoughts as if on a screen, but to no avail. Painful and innocuous thoughts alike streamed through his mind: It's no use ... My foot's itchy ... I'll never get better ...

He let out a throaty growl and returned to his breathing.

Like clouds, he reminded himself.

He breathed, felt his breath, felt the gentle way in which it expanded his chest. In a flash, like the lightning of the Divine, whatever that Divine may be, he saw a thought emerge from his subconscious, from blackness. It was fluffy and dark — "I feel pain" — and he was looking at that thought. He saw, or felt, that it had massive weight, emotional weight. But as it moved across the horizon of his consciousness, he did not feel one way or the other about it. He just saw it. There it was, and there it went. It disappeared into blackness from which it had come. His mind ignited. He saw that the thought was not exactly true. In that moment he was rather okay. Other thoughts emerged from the blackness.

I'm cold ...

What time is it?

I'm hurt ...

He watched the thoughts emerge like clouds and move across his mind. He watched the emotions that went with them.

What is this?!

Around this thought, this thought in particular, was space. A sliver of space — a space of neutrality, of pure observation. In that space Philip found relief, a relief he had not felt in months, a peace and a balance. He paused for a moment looking at that space, delving in it, and then:

It exploded.

It became a galaxy of peace that permeated his mind and sank into his soul.

Philip snapped his eyes open. He looked out the window at the inky red leaves glowing under the sun. He did not know what he had just experienced or how long it would last. But a seed had been planted. A seed of something critical, something hot — like the knowledge that the sun drives all life, something that infallible.

At that moment none of that mattered to him. He felt relief. Sun poured into the room. He could have jumped up and shaken everyone's hand. Instead, he breathed and drank deeper still.

[CHAPTER ONE]

Paying attention in a particular way: on purpose,
in the present moment, and nonjudgmentally.

— Jon Kabat-Zinn

I stood in front of the mirror, looking into my own eyes. My pupils were dilated. They fractionally pulsed open and closed, and I knew I was ill.

I gripped the edge of the sink until my knuckles were bone-white. How could I be ill again?

Truth struck me irrefutably when I looked into my own eyes, the way I could see any truth, simple or complex, when I looked into the eyes of another. I heard the truth there as though it were the song of the symphonic choir of Beethoven's 9th.

We all have hundreds of sensors that inform us when someone speaks the truth. They are both conscious and unconscious, and are like tentacles, or probes, from our mind, seeking the correct ports in another mind.

The sheer number of these probes makes the system nearly impossible to fool. Though we are not all in tune with this, we are familiar with the results: a gut feeling, or feelings of trust or distrust. Long ago I'd discovered something of a knack in myself for this particular faculty, something I did not often share, something I preferred to keep private, but something that has proven useful.

The most important of these sensors is the eyes. Oh, the eyes! We all know the power of the eyes. If I want to tell if someone is speaking the truth, I look into his or her eyes, let everything else fade into the background, and listen. Not just to the words, but to the language of the eyes. When I looked now into my own eyes, hot steam beading on my skin, I listened to their song, without judgment, unclouded by bias, and I knew the truth.

"How, after all this time could I be ill again? Eh, Philip? How?" I said again to the man in mirror.

I was aware that the diagnosis I had been plagued with could flare up at any time. But for the last year, especially the last few months, I had felt fine. Better than fine — great.

Too great?

That thought came like a lightning bolt from a black sky over a stormy ocean. Usually, standing in my bathroom, with its green stone tiles and soft terry-cloth bathmat, I could picture myself standing in the moors of England; the mat tickled the soles of my feet like that rolling terrain's mosses. Today, with the steam trapped in that small bathroom and swirling around me, I felt more like I was standing on the moors of hell.

I shook my thoughts away and padded down the cool hallway to my bedroom. I pulled out a pressed white shirt and a grey herringbone suit. The suit had baby-blue pinstripes, and I thought it to look quite smart. I buttoned the shirt and pulled on the jacket, the cotton of the shirt grating against the silk of jacket sleeve, its sound like sandpaper drawn over steel in the quiet of the bedroom. As I pulled on the other sleeve, my bicep muscles gave that bittersweet feeling of being well used. The sensation drew my thoughts to my morning training at the aikido dojo. I felt a sting of guilt. The art, at its root, is the Art of Peace. Instead of treating my partner's disrespect as a challenge, I'd responded in kind, and then with more ferocity. It was not the Way. A layer of myself was troubled by my actions, even though the guy had been asking for it. As I contemplated the experience, I wondered, was it the intensity of the exercise that caused my eyes to behave this way?

I seized onto that one thought, the one truth-port not yet activated, like a piece of flotsam after a shipwreck. I snapped on my watch, a stainless-steel chronograph. The crack of the latch secured the thought in my mind. I buttoned my jacket, the tailored fabric hugging my waist like a girdle of armor, and I stepped down the hallway and into the woods.

———————

Earlier that morning, walking into the stark white bamboo-trimmed dojo, Philip noted as usual the simplicity of the place, a simplicity achieved through great effort. In the morning session, he was paired with a man two or three years his senior. Aikido is the art of redirecting another's energy with minimal effort, so Philip was surprised when his partner came at him forcefully, making the movements, the grappling and throwing, with great effort. Grunting and sweating, he attempted to overcome Philip's attacks with force. Initially, finding this humorous, Philip allowed himself to be guided along by his partner's movements, thinking he would give up the use of force when he realized that it was unnecessary and counterproductive. But Philip's partner did not get the message. Time and again the two men squared off in their impeccably white gi, and time and again the other man attempted to muscle Philip around the mats. A kind of annoyance, a disrespect, began to build in Philip.

Tiring of his partner's inability to conceptually grasp the message, Philip faced him again, planted his feet on the ground, and raised his arms in ready position.

His partner stepped in, swinging his arm down from above in a head strike.

Philip blended with the attack, grasped his partner's wrist, stepped lightly under his arm, pivoted, and guided the man's arm gently down. This movement unbalanced the attacker and bent him double at the waist. There he stood, arm above his back, bent double, expecting the completion of the throw, but Philip held him still, not permitting him to move forward or back.

Eventually his partner turned his head up and back, unnaturally, to glance at Philip. Philip returned the gaze, as though to say, "Look how I can hold you with little to no force. I could hold you here all day and there would be nothing you could do about it." Philip took a step forward, releasing the arm, and his partner rolled safely down to the mat.

Philip smiled as he walked away and adjusted his gi, thinking that a balance had been engendered in their practice. But on the next throw, Philip's partner came doubly fast, doubly hard. He again tried to muscle and push Philip's two hundred pounds around the floor. Philip was not amused.

He squared up, inviting an attack. His partner came fast, swinging his arm down at Philip's head. Philip again blended with his arm, grasping his wrist, and again stepped lightly under his arm. But this time he stepped deep, past his partner's centre and, in conjunction, fluidly rotated around his own core, changing direction like the torrent of a river bending around a rock. This unbalanced his partner, who, in an instinctual move, attempted to grasp Philip's wrist for support.

As he grabbed at Philip's sleeve, Philip stepped past him again. And as the man began to fall, Philip snapped his arms, wrists, and hands in a viciously quick movement into line with his centre — exponentially accelerating the fall mid-air. Philip moved so fast that everything else seemed to slow down. He watched as beads of sweat from his partner's face seemed to travel vertically toward the ceiling.

Whumpht!

His partner hit the mat squarely between his shoulder blades, his legs where his head should have been. The sound, echoing through the dojo, sought some object to muffle it, some colour to mute it, and finding none in that stark whiteness it rang out as though the dojo were the mouth of an ancient bell.

_____

I stepped past my desk in the living room under the front window and paused by the door. Light reflected off the water through the window and illuminated the pages on my desk.

I lived with my uncle in Toronto, in a townhouse that overlooked a small harbour and two yacht clubs. Both my uncle and I belonged to the larger of the two, the Toronto Yacht Club. Besides being a great place to store my boat, it made for a convenient spot for a cocktail.

I'd moved back in with my uncle like a boomerang after a failed experiment in living with a woman. And after, perhaps oddly, something of a windfall. My grandfather had left me a small amount of money. The cheque had come in the spring, and even though I was twenty-five, I'd moved back in with my uncle. It was difficult to explain to friends why I'd done this, but the root of the decision revolved around the fact that I wanted to write poetry. I knew there was no money to be made in such a pursuit, but I figured if I was careful with my money, I could make it last a year and focus full-time on my writing. So I left that shattered relationship, chalking it up to a bad match, quit my job with an engineering firm, and moved back in.

I figured I could take this time to start on my work, get the wheels moving, maybe even put together a small book of poems before I'd have to go back to work. It had been worth it, even though things had been strained with my uncle as of late.

But something had been going wrong. I could not bring myself to look at the lines of poetry that ran over the stark white pages. The lines began well, but as I drove to the core of the words, my mind would begin to scatter, and I would push the pages away in frustration. The white couch across the room was littered with pricks of blue ink where I'd thrown my pen across the room.

In the last weeks it had gotten worse; I could barely get a line of words out. That was not all. A lover of books, I could hardly read a paragraph before my attention fluttered like a moth in a hurricane. Perhaps that was my first hint that something was wrong. I bristled at the thought and shoved it out of my head. To soothe my mind, I turned to thought of my sailboat, received in adjunct to my cash windfall. A beautiful J/24, a stripped-down all-out racer. An image of her gleaming white hull mellowed in my mind.

I locked the door behind me and trod down the boardwalk to the club. It had been a great place in its heyday. Now it was little more than a home for floating cottages, boats stuck cheek by jowl. The decor of the club itself was intended to be sophisticated but came off phony. Frankly, it looked more like a Swiss Chalet than a yacht club.

As I walked into the high-windowed room overlooking the harbour, several people glanced up. This was a normal phenomenon. It seemed a prerequisite of membership was a perverse curiosity about everyone else's business.

I spotted my uncle at the bar wearing a dark suit and looking gentlemanly as usual with his trim grey goatee. I crossed the restaurant, and by habit took a survey of the women in the club as I went.

"I think I'm sick," I said, settling on a stool beside him.

He turned to me with a half-raised eyebrow. "I'm glad you've come to that conclusion. You now have the opportunity to do something about it. You've caught it in time."

"You think so?" I said, exhaling deeply the mixture of emotions within me. An attractive young woman wearing a red tie came up behind the bar. It was pleasant to see Stephanie wearing that tie. I'd given it to her a week before, because I noticed that she was always wearing a different boldly coloured tie. And also because I'd slept with her. I ordered a rum and Coke.

"It's been years," he continued, "since you were first hit with it and none of us knew what it was then. We — you, I, and everyone who cares for you — had never heard of bipolar disorder, except peripherally."

"Whoa, whoa. Bipolar disorder?" I said, pressing the flat of my palm against the granite bar. "Who said anything about that? Depression. That's what I had. How many times do I have to tell you?" This had been a bone of contention between us for some time. I had been through a difficult and dangerous depression, and while I had been down and unable to defend myself, my uncle had taken me to a doctor who had diagnosed me with bipolar disorder. I hardly even knew what that was. The doctor had not even bothered to explain it to me before he scratched off a prescription.

The recollection set me on edge. When I had met the doctor, I had felt like I was underwater. Everything was distant and disorientated. I remember trying to ask the doctor to explain, but he had waved my quiet, quivering question away. Then he had reached into his desk drawer, pulled out a Polaroid camera, snapped a picture of me — without my permission, without a word — and stapled it to the outside of my file. I remember watching as he flipped through a file-cabinet drawer near where I sat. Dozens of frightened, haggard faces had peered back at my from their steel incarceration before he dropped in my file and clanked the drawer shut. Who even has a Polaroid camera these days? I'd thought. I never went back, and if I ever saw that doctor again, he would be lucky to just get a piece of my mind.

Yet my uncle seemed to agree with the diagnosis. He was wrong.

"We all had to learn what it was, and believe me," my uncle said, "I know you have had to learn what it is about and deal with the derailment. I can't imagine what it takes to deal with that. And I have been right beside you through all this." He rubbed his grey goatee. "The one thing that is certain is that you have the ability to take control of this thing — before the train leaves the station."

I barely heard him as I watched Stephanie's hips sway down the length of the bar. When I reconnected with what he was saying, I was irked. That struck me as odd, for it had been me who'd brought up the subject.

"I suppose that's true," I said, forcing my tone to stay even. If the train hasn't already left the station, I added to myself.

"It's so simple." He took a deep breath. "Philip — take the pills. Call your doctor, don't wait, and take the medicine. That's all there is to it."

"What do you know of it?" I hissed. "Simple, is it? Have you no conception of what you are saying? You sit there and glibly discuss the very basis of thought and emotion, the very basis of cognition. There is nothing, *nothing* simple about it." My uncle stared at me. If he was startled by my outburst, he gave no indication.

Stephanie rolled up to the bar and delivered my rum and Coke with a cock of her head, her long, straight black hair falling away from her face, shielding her gaze from unwanted observers. Behind the curtain of her raven hair, she favoured me with a smile.

I flashed her a half-smile in that tunnel of intimacy and gathered up my drink.

"Of course, Philip," ventured my uncle, his speech slow and deliberate. "But you remember the battles you fought. The depression that debilitated you for months, that you had to arm yourself against daily."

"Of course," I said, the wind deserting my sails.

"... the time studying meditation, what that has taught you, your time in the hospital. The mania that almost consumed you —"

I slammed my glass down on the bar in a manner engineered to smack his eardrums but not to draw attention from the other patrons. I had suffered from depressions, each one more difficult and more dangerous, true — the last particularly bad. And when it was over, anything that made me feel good, well, it was good with me. But mania, no. Perhaps I partied a little too much, drank a little too much. But ...

"Consume me?" I said, evenly, quietly. You cocksucker, I wanted to add. "Time in the hospital? Time spent there at *your* behest. Let me ask you something. Why is it whenever things begin to go well for me, when I begin to gather some measure of independence, you accuse me of being ill?" I was not entirely sure where that statement came from, but the anger I found in my system was inexplicable and undeniable.

"What are talking about, Philip?" he said, and pressed the bridge of his nose between his thumb and forefinger.

"You know very well what I am talking about. I certainly don't have spell it out to you. I'm telling you, you'd better back off." I straightened my back and inhaled. "I'm going for a cigarette," I said, and finished my drink in a single swig. I walked out the side door onto the restaurant patio and into the brilliant clear sun and cool breezy air.

A woman who looked vaguely familiar leaned against the railing, her long blonde hair curling in the wind. To distract myself from my roiling anger, I went over to strike up a conversation.

As I approached, recognition sparkled in my mind. Heather glanced up as I approached. I'd met her at the last sailing regatta, in Rochester, New York, the weekend before. Her small frame and large bosom coupled with her blonde hair made for a potent mix. I'd started chatting her up at the regatta for no more reason than that Frankie, a guy who I was sailing with, had asked me, after more than a couple of beers, "How do you pick up women?" I'd had to laugh at that one, for I am no expert on the subject, and Frankie was at least approaching forty if not older. Had he had no opportunity to examine the issue for himself in all his time on the planet? That conversation had taken an unexpected turn.

Now I took in the view of downtown Toronto, the harbour, the island airport, and the lake beyond. The boats in the harbour bobbed below, eager for their masters to let them loose. I slowed my pace and leaned up on the railing beside her. She turned and smiled softly.

"Is that your boat?" she asked.

I realized she had been looking down at the dry-sail yard, where the race boats were stored on land, just below the patio. I looked over the railing and my heart accelerated at the sight of my boat resting in her cradle, her bluff bow striking out for the heavens. I admired her immaculate white hull, adorned with a single red racing stripe. The boat was a J/24, a balls-to-the-wall racer whose pedigree I had contributed to with many victories in international Great Lake regattas.

"That's her, all right," I said. "*Falconry*."

"*Falconry*. That's a little bit of a strange name. Why's she called that?"

"Well, *Falcon* is a common name for boats — bird of prey and all that. Falconry, the art of hunting with a falcon, seemed to suit a race boat."

"I see," she said, gazing at the boat.

"But we call her *Falcon* for short." I smiled. "I'll take you out sometime if you like?"

"Mmm." She whipped around and stared intently at me. "I've been thinking a lot about our last conversation. I'd like you ... to call me." She pulled a card from pocket with designed precision.

I received the card with a slight bow, not breaking eye contact.

- Heather Ridley -

Fiction Inc. Films

Post-Production - Editing Division

V. P.

I read the card and looked up. She was blushing.

"Our last ... conversation?" I said playfully.

"Walk me to my car?" she asked.

"My pleasure."

I followed her down, watching the swell of her backside as we manoeuvred the steps. The view produced that warm feeling in my belly, and I wondered if she had come to the club just to see me. It is not often that one has a card so close at hand. Usually it requires time to produce one from a case or wallet, and I could not see anyone who was asking for her attention to say goodbye.

We stopped in front of a black BMW X3. Of course she drives a BMW, I thought. Nice cars to be sure, and in the '70s a far less common car and even considered exotic. These days, though, to my mind, they were something of a cliché.

We had not spoken since we left the patio, and finally she said, "How did you do at the regatta last weekend?"

"We got the ace —" She stepped into me and pressed her soft lips up into mine, probing, seeking pleasure. Her bosom pressed into my chest, making it bigger still as as she sought to close the distance between us. The light smell of tangerine clouded my senses.

She broke off the kiss and looked me in the eye.

"Call me," she said, and turned and jumped up into her truck.

I walked back to *Falconry* and patted her hull. "What you think of *that*, eh, *Falcon*?"

———

The circumstances of the race had been last minute. Philip had been loitering around the townhouse when the phone rang.

"Mate, it's Frank," came the voice over the phone. Frank — or, as Philip sometimes called him to bust his chops, Frankie — was an old friend of Philip's, and though he did not own a boat, he often asked Philip to sail with him.

"Frankie, how goes?"

"Yeah, not bad. Listen. I was scheduled to be in a regatta next week in the States. The boat I was going to drive dropped out. I wanted to know if you were interested in taking your J

down to New York for an international race. I got two other guys looking forward to it. We'd be short-handed by one, but what the heck. You game?"

Philip looked at the phone for a moment.

"Sounds interesting," he said.

"We could take my truck, trailer the boat down. It's a big competition, we do well, would be good for my record."

Frankie was an international J/24 racer, a Canadian champion, and a nice guy to boot.

"Short one, though, Frankie," Philip said. "You want to compete like that?"

"No worries — our fourth is a big guy, pushing two-fifty."

Philip considered. The J had a huge amount of sail area for the size of the boat. It took a crew of five people to counteract the force of the sails. The J moved fastest when she was sailing flat. The large force of the wind tended to heel the boat on its side, destroying the hull hydrodynamics. If the fourth who Frankie suggested was approaching two-fifty, that was almost the weight of two smaller sailors, and being short a crew member would be negligible. And a trip to the States for an international sailing race would be fun. Besides, what else am I doing this weekend? thought Philip.

"I like it," he said into the handset.

"Right on, mate."

"In fact, buddy, let's rock out with our Bach out."

"That's funny, you're a funny guy."

* * *

That Saturday, Philip, Frankie, and two others, MacGillis and Bill, powered out of the harbour in Rochester on the J. The morning sun was burning off the fog that lay over the still water of the harbour, and brought with it a fresh breeze. Philip could sense the lake's choppy waters beyond the grey opaqueness of the fog and the stillness of the harbour's isolated waters.

The forecast called for strong winds, the same winds that had whipped up the lake during the night, and the coming intensity could be felt in the rapidity of the breeze's escalation.

Twenty other boats powered out of the harbour in an ordered line. Some flew flags emblazoned with team crests; others blared music from their sound systems, mostly '70s rock. Philip could not help but smile at the different race psychologies. It all humoured him, for all of this mattered little when the boats hit the line.

Philip wore a white long-sleeved microfibre top (to keep the unrelenting sun off and offset the chill of the upwind legs of the race), khaki shorts, and a white cap. He cast an eye over his crew members. Frankie looked spry and tanned as usual in a dark blue polo. Their foredeck man, Bill, was small and thin, perfect for the position, where low weight and high agility were required. Bill was in his mid-forties, his shiny bald head revealing a protruding forehead.

The final crew member was, true to Frankie's word, a huge two-hundred-fifty-pound Scotsman, and not a little of his weight was muscle. Though MacGillis was not very experienced, he appeared keen and game for some fun. He was sitting on the rail, legs swung over the side, and Philip noted the efficient manner in which he coiled the dock lines.

As soon as Falconry powered out of the little sheltered bay in which the harbour was nestled, the boat was assailed by large swells; the little three-horsepower outboard began to struggle to keep her on course.

Philip steered a course that took the wakes of the port quarter, rolling with the swells instead of attempting to power through them. After a few minutes he turned the helm over to Frankie, as they had agreed. Frankie wanted to gain more experience on the helm and improve his record. Philip would run the cockpit, call tactics, run the jib, and organize the others in the crew. As Philip handed the tiller over to Frankie he said in low voice, "You know you have trouble with downwind in heavy seas. You going to be able to handle it?"

"Not a problem, mate. I got this."

Philip nodded and took up his position in the cockpit, gathered up the jib lines, one multi-coloured high-tech line in each hand, and called, "Okay boys, lets do it to it. Ready on the jib."

"Roger," called Bill from the foredeck, scampering from his seat on the rail. He braced himself against the shrouds and made up the tension of the jib halyard. He looked back at Philip, and Philip gave him a nod. Bill bent over and pulled on the halyard, hand over hand, using his entire wingspan to pull the halyard through the mast. The jib shot up the *forestay, its white high-tech fabric blocking out a perfect triangle of blue sky.*

Frankie drove the boat into the eye of the wind and MacGillis and Bill unlashed the mainsail and repeated the hoisting procedure. Both sails beat noisily in the wind. Frankie twisted over the stern and killed the engine.

Frankie leaned the tiller over, and the bow gently fell off the wind. Philip made up on the jib sheet, the ratchet block clicking in mathematical perfection. The sails caught, and the boat leapt forward. In the absence of the drone of the engine and the banging of the sails, all that could be heard was the song of the blue water racing down the hull.

They did not have long to enjoy the quiet, for barely a minute after the sails had been raised, a loud bang from the committee boat cannon signalled five minutes to the start.

Philip swept his gaze over the fleet. Already the boats were jockeying for position, tailing each other, tacking, jibbing, all vying for the best position at the start. Frankie drove the boat hard for the line.

Another boat, with the right of way, drove down on them from the port side.

"Tacking!" called Frankie. He laid the helm hard over and the boat sprang through the wind; Philip released the port sheet, wrapped the starboard sheet around the winch, and ferociously pulled the sheet through its blocks so that the jib jumped through the wind. Bill and MacGillis shifted from the port to the starboard rail as the boat came onto course. The sails filled on the opposite tack, and the J accelerated at what

seemed to Philip to be an almost exponential rate. She drove off the top of a wave hovered there for a moment and then the bow dove down into the hollow of the trough — her stern rode out the wave and her bow drove up to take the next wave. The boat that had been bearing down on them passed their stern within metres.

"Atta girl," Philip muttered.

The gun signalling two minutes banged in the background.

"Whatta you think?" Philip heard Frankie say to his back.

Philip looked around. Almost all the boats were jockeying about the start boat, trying to get as close to it as possible, for there lay a small advantage.

"I know the boat is favoured," he said, "but there are too many boats in here. Let's ditch it, head for the pin and clear air."

"Really?" said Frankie. This went against conventional wisdom.

"Absolutely."

Frankie snapped his head around, taking in the environment, and drove the boat straight to the line. Before crossing, they tacked again and drove the boat along the line, away from the mass of boats.

"Ballsy," said Frankie.

"One minute," called Bill from the foredeck, shiny head bent over his wristwatch.

Still they drove for the other end of line. Off their port quarter Philip spotted another boat.

He cursed under his breath.

"Okay, Frankie," he said. "Lay off the line a little — we got another guy coming in. We're going to have to hit the line at full speed or he's going to steal our wind and our position and all our advantage will be lost."

"Thirty seconds," called Bill.

"Got it," said Frankie, and he adjusted the course to put some space between the line and the boat. Philip watched as the other boat adjusted course to head for the exact spot he intended to cross the line. They were now on a collision course. Philip caught a look pass between MacGillis and Bill.

"Okay, Frankie," he said. "When I call it, head up hard for the line. We'll flip on this guy, steal his wind, and cross the line."

"Ten seconds."

The boats were thirty metres apart. The wind was raging, the water swelled under the boat, and foam leapt along her hull. A rogue wave caught the bow and spray shot over the foredeck, drenching Bill. He did not look up from his watch.

"Wait for it," said Philip.

"Let's see what you got, Falcon," said Frankie into the teeth of the wind.

"Oh, she's got it," tossed Philip over his shoulder. The boats were twenty metres apart, three boat lengths. Then ten metres. The freedom of blue water between them was being eaten up.

"Head up! Trim for speed."

Frankie laid the tiller hard over and fully trimmed in the main sail. Philip ground in the winch hard, trimming the jib to a stiff wing shape that more resembled a blade.

It was as though someone had tossed a dime in the water and said, "Here, turn on that." She careened around her centre: drove her keel deep into the water, transferred her momentum to centrifugal force, turned around her keel, and transferred her momentum to forward velocity; her sails ate up the wind, and she accelerated like a demon chased by divine providence.

"Two. One," came the count from the foredeck.

BANG!

The committee boat cannon signalled the start.

With her nose in clear wind, her bow cutting the blue water, Falconry steadily dropped the competitor's boat. First half a boat length, then one boat length, then two, and she was away, driving out ahead of the fleet. Philip looked astern at the other boat. A brunette in yellow sailing pants sat on the rail staring at them, her jaw slack. Philip gave her a little wave and then took in the fleet — all the boats lined up, prettily giving chase.

"Son of a bitch," said Frankie into the wind.

They won that race, got the bullet — the "ace" — and placed second in the next race and first again in the third, giving them the silverware to take home, and, more importantly, Frankie his stats for his record.

* * *

After the races, Frankie and Philip were having a beer, and not their first. It was dark at Irondequoit New York Yacht Club, the patio bar illuminated by strings of hanging lights.

"Sweet one, eh?" said Philip.

"Yup," replied Frankie, swaying gently, his eyes glassed over. "What do you think of those two?"

Philip followed his gaze toward two women who grasped plastic beer cups and talk in low tones to each other.

"Those two? Fine, I guess."

"Fine! Fine? Damn right, fine. They're fucking beautiful."

Philip looked again — a blonde and a brunette. The brunette Philip recognized from the fist race, and was nothing special. She wore her wind-tussled hair in a tight ponytail that did nothing for her pudgy cheeks. The other, the blonde, wore tight yoga pants and a black zip-up sweater. He couldn't see what was under the sweater, but the yoga pants sure did something for her visible figure.

She flicked up her eyes to meet his, and a little smile tugged at the corner of her mouth. Something electric flashed through the space between them. Philip felt that thing tugging at his belly, and the woman broke off the look — but not her smile, which she directed instead into her cup as she took a sip.

"You know what?" said Frankie, slapping Philip's shoulder and sloshing beer in the process. "You should show me how to pick up women."

"What," said Philip, "makes you think I know more about picking up women than you? I'm probably half your age."

"Puph! I'm not that old. Come on, man, show me."

Philip looked at him askew. The truth was — and anyone who knew anything about women knew this — it's ladies' choice. But of course there was nothing wrong with letting those not in the know think otherwise. "Fine," he said. "Follow me."

He took a swig of his beer and casually pointed a curving course toward the blonde. He stopped a few paces behind her. The brunette tilted her head and looked Philip up and down.

"Hi," said Frankie, darting out from behind Philip.

"Hi," replied the brunette, her voice taut, like it had been thrown into the circle by a ventriloquist. The blonde turned and gave Philip a smile, her soft pink lips distracting him for a moment. All he could think was that they had the appearance of moisture without actually being wet.

Philip opened his mouth to speak, but before he could, Frankie swayed and stepped into the middle of the circle, thrusting his hand toward the brunette.

"I'm Frank, or sometimes people call me Frankie, I don't really know why, I think it sounds gay ... but not like, you know, homosexual gay, but fun gay ..."

"Sally," said the brunette, taking his hand, and Philip watched as her lips pursed up. They literally did that, pursed up, making her lips look like some shrivelled prune, too long in the sun.

Internally, Philip shuddered.

He turned to the blonde. Humour twinkled at the corners of her eyes, and Philip found himself delighted by her equanimity.

"So, you wanna go for a walk?" he said.

"Sure."

Philip bent his head in a curtailed bow, and they stepped off into the night. Reaching the edge of the light thrown by strings of lightbulbs that hung over the dance floor, Philip looked back over his shoulder. Frankie and the brunette stood shoulder to shoulder, plastic beer jugs in hand, looking back at them, expressionless. Philip gave Frankie a little shrug and followed the blonde off into the warm night.

* * *

In the illusion of privacy created by the darkness surrounding the dance floor, the blonde unzipped her sweater, revealing a bosom that almost had Philip forgetting where he was. All he could see was the glow of her blonde hair and the skin above her pink tank top. The fabric seemed to be in a losing battle to contain what lay beneath.

"Christ ..." Philip muttered.

"Pardon?" asked the blonde.

"The race, did you watch the race?" Philip asked, forcing himself to look her squarely in the eyes and hoping his stupid grin did not transfer across the dimness.

"I did," she said. "Some friends brought me down from Toronto — they were on the judges' boat, and I got to go along for the ride. I watched the entire race from there."

"Nice. I was racing today."

"I know. I saw you out there."

"Ahh," said Philip.

They found a smooth piece of driftwood that had been hauled out of the harbour, its gnarled branches snapped short on its long journey to its current resting place.

"I'm Heather," said the blonde, sitting on the sun-baked wood.

"Philip," Philip replied, settling beside her. The night was warm and the wind still. The lights of the clubhouse and the dock lights reflected off the water.

"So, you're from Toronto too, eh?" asked Philip. "What club are you from?"

"The Toronto Yacht Club. Do you know it?"

"I do," said Philip, laughing. "I've been a member since I wore short pants. I can't believe I've never seen you there before."

"Well, I'm a new member. Only a month now. I've been looking for a new activity, and my friends suggested sailing. I have to say I love it. The people are great, and I love being out on the water. This was my first time seeing the big boys in action. Oh, and the club — I love it. Great patio, and the restaurant is beautiful."

"Yeah ..." said Philip. He took a sip of his beer and wondered if they were talking about the same restaurant.

Philip, having lost a beat, caused the conversation to lapse into silence. Music drifted over to them from the dance floor, a classic soul song sung by five drunk white guys. For a moment he was afraid he had lost the thread entirely, that he was going to douse the opportunity, but it appeared that Heather was at least as determined as he.

"Tell me something you have never told anyone before," she said.

"Pardon?"

"Tell me something you have never told anyone before ... I can't stand meaningless chit chat, get-to-know-you bullshit. Tell me something personal." Philip raised his eyebrows and thought. His head swam and he realized he was far more drunk than he had thought.

Later he would wonder what had possessed him to be so revealing with this woman, someone he did not know. Perhaps it was her figure, or the trust that seemed to run through her smile, or the cocoon of darkness solidified by alcohol. But most likely it was the directness of the question and the fact the he too had little patience for small talk.

He took a large hit of ale and looked for something interesting in the bottom of his cup.

"They say I have a bipolar disorder," he said. "I don't exactly know what that means, and I suppose I've had my fair share of depression. But I'll tell you one thing: there is nothing more exasperating than some asshole doctor telling you you have something and then doing nothing to explain what it is, or how it affects you, then prescribing some pills and

disappearing." *Philip gritted his teeth.* "I don't know, I'm not quite convinced of the whole thing, and it seems my uncle — he raised me — is intent on hammering the issue every chance he gets."

Philip looked off into the harbour, the opened wound's swirling made more potent by the booze and the thought that perhaps he had said too much. Heather was quiet and looked at Philip's profile in the half-light.

"I can't have children," *she said.*

"Pardon?" *said Philip.*

"I can't have children ... anymore."

Philip waited.

"I discovered it two years ago. My ex and I had been living together and trying to get pregnant for over a year. We both went for fertility testing and, well, it was a long and difficult process." *Her eyes softened, and she peered into the middle distance.*

"Finally I did get pregnant," *she continued,* "but ... we lost the the baby."

"Fuck," *said Philip, suddenly stone cold sober.*

"No," *she said.* "It wasn't meant to be. But it was hard. We could have tried again, but I don't think either of us were interested in going through it. All the tests, the doctors, making love on a schedule ... It drained us both."

Philip stared over the dark water.

"He left me soon after," *she said.* "And that's what hurts. Not the leaving — I know that was the right thing, we fought constantly. But still ... If you can believe it, eight months later he already has a girl pregnant. Twenty-three, she is. Disgusting. I don't look that old, do I?" She smiled at him then, and Philip was sure that the smile had every intention of conveying humour. Instead, she looked determined ... and sad. The intimacy of it began to congeal something in him. He felt the beginnings of a bond form.

"Why, how old are you?" he asked.

"Thirty-five," she said, her eyes on Philip.

"Not that old at all, then," he said. "Only a decade older than me."

She giggled, the sound was light and bubbly. "Oddly," she said, her eyes flashing in the dark, "I'm happier than I have ever been."

After a time Philip said, "I suppose we all have a cross to bear. And when we take up that weight, see things how they actually are, there is a type of freedom."

A smile lit her face and spread to her eyes. She slid along the log, closing the space between them to a few inches.

"Did you ever think perhaps he was just not the right person for you?" Philip went on, attempting to ignore her movement. "There is so much we don't know. I've heard that women who think they can't get pregnant sometimes, in their forties, find themselves suddenly with child, and often this happens with a new partner ... someone more suited to them."

"You're a lot wiser than your age suggests," she said.

"I get that a lot," said Philip.

Heather looked at him then. He could not be sure, but he thought he saw a blush rise in her pale, moonlit cheeks.

"What I am doing?" she said. "A twenty-five-year-old sailor! My gosh, I can't. I cannot sleep with you."

"Oh —" said Philip, glancing away. "No, I would never think that."

"Never?" she said, with a pantomime of a pout.

Philip let out a stream of air and stared up to the heavens.

She leaned in hard and pressed her lips into his. Heat radiated off the space between her bosom and her sweater. As Philip pressed his lips back into hers, he opened his eyes and glanced downed at the cavernous space between her breasts. He felt he could fall into it, coddled in pleasure.

"Yikes," he said, breaking off the kiss.

"Yikes?" giggled Heather.

"Sorry. Sometimes I become inarticulate when the blood leaves my brain." And he did feel like that, swooning in heat and the light scent of her perfume. Tangerine?

"Umhh," she grabbed the front of his shirt with both hands and pulled him into her again. Her kiss was fierce, but her tongue gently probed at his half-open mouth, trying to pull more pleasure from him.

"Well, sailor," she breathed into his mouth. "I feel like being bad."

"Bad, eh?"

"What do you say you go grab us a couple more drinks and meet me over there." She gestured back with her head at the workshop, tucked into the darkest corner of the property.

Philip stood up from their driftwood bench. He towered over her, her face at his waistline, and stared at her golden hair and oval eyes filled with heat. "What are you having? Will gin do the trick?"

"Make it a double, sailor," she said, her eyes flicking down to his waist.

Philip nearly passed out.

"Four minutes, by the workshop," he said. She nodded, and in the darkness he could not be sure but he thought he saw the tip of her pink tongue run over her engorged lips.

Philip disengaged from her aura and broke into the circle of light that was the party. Drunken sailors stomped on the dance floor and clusters of people hooted and laughed under strings of lights. The band closed a song, and in the silence Philip could hear the mast chimes, taut ropes banging masts, singing over the harbour.

Honesty: I will have to remember to tell Frankie that particular technique for picking up woman, thought Philip. He spied Frankie talking to MacGillis in a corner and moved quickly to avoid his attention.

He ordered two double gin and tonics at the bar and tried to ignore what he imagined was the bartender's knowing smile. He took a sip of the bitter lime fluid. Its flavour and coldness momentarily sobered him before driving his thoughts deeper into a lustful haze.

He moved toward the edge of the party and glanced over to where Frankie and MacGillis were standing. Frankie shot his arm up and made a move toward him. Philip raised a hand holding a glass to his neck and made a cutting motion with his thumb: the universal "no go" sign. Frankie stopped short with a confused look, made humorous by his glassed-over eyes, and Philip slipped out of the light.

Philip picked his way into the dark corner of the club. The scent of freshly cut grass sweetened the air. He could see only the outline of the workshop and the twinkle of stars above it. Gradually he saw the light hue of Heather's hair and her outline, barely visible against the building behind her.

"Here you go, good looking," he said. She looked coyly back at him and blinked her sparkling eyes in the night.

"Will you hold these for me?" she asked, as she took the drink from him.

Philip could not see what she pressed into his hand in the darkness. It felt rough against the pads of his fingers but had a silken softness. He hooked his thumb under a strap and let a pair of thong panties fall. As recognition sparked in him, blood shot into his member, steeling him and forcing it to strain against the fabric of his pants.

"I love sex," she said, moving into him in the darkness. "I love everything about it, but most of all I love to be wet, and I'm wet now ..."

[CHAPTER TWO]

Know such thoughts to be claws fraught with poison.

— Rumi, *The Sage and the Peacock*

The next morning I woke with a hangover, and the morning after that, and the morning after that. In fact, for the week after I spoke with my uncle, waking with a hangover became a habit.

One evening during this time, after what was now my customary tenth rum and Coke, the bartender, Stephanie, had tried to cut me off. I'd spoken roughly with her, informing her, "This is how sailors drink."

Though I affected not to care, the incident stayed with me, for no one had attempted to cut me off since I was in high school. This was compounded by the fact that Stephanie and I had a history, and I'd never known her to be vindictive.

Two days later, I arrived at the yacht club needing to purge myself, to clear my head — needing to sail.

It was a beautiful day. The sun was shining, the sky was a deep indigo blue, and the breeze was light and steady. The weather only reaffirmed my desire to be on the water.

Today I lacked a crew to move my boat over to the launching crane. I also lacked the desire to muscle two tons of boat around myself. My uncle and I had many friends at the club, though. As a favour, my uncle had agreed to take care of a friend's boat, a small cruiser, while she was away on holidays overseas. I again felt the breeze — it lifted my hair to a perfect degree — and I decided to borrow the cruiser. The fact that this could be tantamount to stealing whispered away in the wind.

The boat had a few problems with the gasoline engine, but I elected to sail in spite of this. Looking back on this decision later, I wondered what had possessed me. It was something I'd never do — take someone else's boat, and one that had a problem with the gas engine at that. It was wrong and dangerous — dangerous in the extreme. If nothing else, it was unseamanlike.

Despite this, I stopped briefly by my own boat and grabbed my radio and life jacket. Then I boarded the little aluminum harbour ferry and directed the attendant to the twenty-seven-foot sailboat moored in the harbour.

When the ferry glided up to the waiting boat, I clambered aboard her and removed the plastic cover that shielded the instruments from the weather. A silver key dropped into my waiting hand. I smiled and waved the ferry away. Unlocking the hatch, I dropped into the cabin. The boat had a small kitchen and living area complete with a large table. The table was covered with tools. I opened a metal water flask that sat next to them and was pleased to find the sharp odour of Scotch assail my nostrils. I had to admit, Uncle had style.

I climbed back on deck and opened the cockpit hatches to reveal the gas tank and fuel pump system; the scent of gasoline infused the atmosphere. The problem was obvious. Most boats have diesel engines for the simple reason that diesel engine fumes are not explosive. A boat has many nooks and crannies and closed compartments, though, in which gasoline fumes can become trapped. Should a spark ignite one of these pockets of fumes, the results can be disastrous. I'd seen many pictures of just such an occurrence. The boats looked like they had been struck by a cruise missile.

I had my doubts about whether or not there truly was a leak. Just because there was a scent of gasoline did not necessarily indicate a problem. To dissipate the fumes, I secured the cockpit hatches open and flipped on the blower. I pulled on my inflatable life jacket. With its black shell and thick nylon straps that doubled as a safety harness should one have to lash oneself to a boat, it reminded me of the equipment fighter pilots wear — I felt like I was preparing to get into an X-wing. I grabbed my handheld radio, clipped it onto my harness, and checked for fumes. Smelling almost nothing, I bent to turn the ignition key. As I did, two almost congruent thoughts competed for my conscious attention. The first: If it is my time, then God will take me. The second, snapping on the heels of the first: What a stupid and extremely dangerous thought to act on, even have — do not even think of acting. You are an excellent sailor, cautious and skilled. Even more troubling, you are not religious.

For some reason I could not stop. I felt the silver key in my fingers, the etching of the brand name, and I felt the first thought hold me, and I could not deny it — I turned the ignition key.

No explosion.

The engine turned over and rumbled to life. I sprang out of the cockpit, ran low across the white deck to the bow, and threw off the mooring lines. Running back to the wheel before the boat could fall off course, I engaged the engine and began to weave through the moored boats.

Passing a sleek forty-foot racer-cruiser, I waved to the owner, an old weathered sailor and family friend who was puttering about her decks. I received a wave back but thought it a bit perfunctory. Perhaps Robert did not recognize me, or wondered what I was doing on this boat.

I lined the boat up with the breakwall entrance. As the prop dug in the water and the wheel tensioned under my hand, a fragment of my mind wondered who would do something like this, steal someone else's sailboat. Later, I would learn that this is called disinhibition: the inability to act on what one knows is right, or, more to the point, the inability to connect with one's own sense of right and wrong.

I powered through the stone breakwall and into the sparkling waters of the lake beyond.

* * *

Once beyond the harbour, I shut down the noisy gas engine. The quiet that descended was numbing.

I hauled out the jib, trimmed it in, and steered a course away from the city. Scanning the horizon, I spotted a green sailboat about ten kilometres away. The boat was quite a bit larger than mine and undoubtedly faster, but I set an intercept course, determined to run it down. As I moved deeper into the lake, the wind blew sweetly, a stiff, fresh breeze. I jumped down below and grabbed the flask of Scotch.

Back at the wheel, I took a spot of the golden liquid, which bit pleasingly at the back of my throat. Along with this sensation, I took in the deep blues of the water and the rich green hues of the treed shoreline and thought: I need a woman. I thought of Heather. Perhaps she would enjoy a sail?

I twisted around to look at the city. The jumble of buildings made me slightly nervous, so much hustle and bustle. Not far off the core I spotted a small marina I used to work at in my youth. Having no phone on the boat, I considered going into the marina. I could call Heather, maybe grab lunch while I waited, and *bingo* — Scotch, sailing, and woman. A potent mix by anyone's standards.

I smoothly swung the boat through the wind, jumped out from behind the wheel, and trimmed in the jib. I swung the bow a couple of points off wind. The sails thumped into shape, and the boat slowly grained speed as I headed for port.

* * *

The marina was actually a government-owned project. It hired students to run the gas docks, a restaurant, and marina services. I dropped the jib on deck, and slipped in past the breakwall. To the starboard side were the gas docks. An attendant, a pudgy fellow wearing a wrinkled Australian sun hat, came out of the office and prepared to grab my lines.

"How you doing today?" I called from a few metres off the dock.

I slipped the boat up to the dock and tossed him the lines.

Once the boat was secured I said, "I have to go to the marina office to see about a slip. Take care of this piece of junk for me."

"Yeah, right," said the attendant. He was wearing sunglasses under his wrinkled hat, so I couldn't quite tell if he caught the joke or not.

I turned and walked off toward the office. En route was the restaurant that I remembered well. I seldom ate there when I worked at the marina, but today I thought I would grab a burger and a beer, and then find a phone and call Heather. I knew full well that it was not proper to leave my boat at the small gas dock, but I didn't really care, figuring it would be fine for at least the span of lunch.

The hostess greeted me as I walked in. She was lean, tanned, and young, though the effect was somewhat ruined by gaudy highlights in her straight brown hair.

"Sit wherever you like," she said.

The restaurant was mostly empty. First I took a seat on the patio, then, feeling not quite right, moved into a booth near the bar. The bartender was beautiful, the two waitresses were beautiful, they were all beautiful. But young. I felt, in a way, bad for thinking them attractive, they were so young.

The waitress came and took my order. She was petite with red hair and pale skin, so pale that her hair colour could be nothing but natural. Feeling a deadly pulse that made me uncomfortable, I again moved out onto the patio. By this time I had gotten the impression that the girls were wondering what exactly it was I was doing. In fact, I wondered what I was doing — I couldn't sit still. I smiled at them as I passed the bar. I cared not for their puzzled expressions. If I stayed within proximity, I might start flirting with them, and I did not like the idea of that.

My seat now overlooked the harbour, and as I sat there, memories of the summers I'd spent here trickled through my mind. The waitress came with my beer. A different waitress, thankfully, and not so attractive. She too was tanned, but skinny and slightly bucktoothed.

"How's your day going?" I said.

"Oh, just fine," she replied.

"I used to work here, you know, quite a few years ago."

"Oh yeah?"

"It was some good times, out in that booth right there for many a summer day," I said, gesturing to the white hut that guarded the entrance to the marina.

"Neat," she said, and moseyed back to the bar.

I took a few swigs of my beer, taking in the view. The marina consisted of maybe one hundred and fifty slips, mostly powerboats. As usual, I was slightly disgusted with the sight of them, for generally the people who owned them were not my favourite type. Exhausting that familiar line of thought, I decided to go the washroom before the food arrived.

On the way back, I noticed a small cramped office with a rather haggard-looking fellow hunched over a desk. Thinking of Heather, I poked my head in.

"Hi there, how you doing?" I said.

"Fine," the man replied.

"Do you have a phone I could use for a second?"

The man paused for a second. Evidently it was a strange question.

"No," he said.

"Indeed," I said looking at the phone on the man's desk. I was actually quite offended by the man's perfunctory response.

It's odd to be so offended, I reflected as I walked down the stairs. It was his private office, after all. But there it was: I was as offended as if he had called my mother a prostitute. I grabbed my beer and walked straight up to the bar, where the redheaded waitress sat at the ready talking to the bartender. I took the stool beside her. Smiling at the redhead, I said to the bartender, "Can I join you?"

"Sure," replied the bartender.

"Do you have a phone at the bar I could use?"

"Sure do," said the waitress.

"Great. I was just upstairs and asked if I could use the phone in the office. Your manager told me no. He's a bit of a dick, eh?"

"Ahh, he's all right."

I could see I was getting no support from this angle. My food came and the bartender also brought a phone up from behind the bar. I rang Heather and got her voicemail, left a brief message, and tucked into the burger. I continued to chat with the waitress and the bartender about this and that while eating my burger, which was dry and overcooked. The two other waitresses joined us. Soon the four of us were have a good old time. Halfway through my fries, which by this time I did not want, I heard a voice behind me.

"Excuse me, sir."

"Yes," I said, turning to take in two teenage security guards wearing black polos. They also wore stupid grins that seemed inappropriate for the task they were performing. The effect brought a taste of the absurd to the scene.

"Is that your boat at the gas docks?"

"It is, yes," I said.

"We need you to move it. We need the space at the dock."

"Fair enough, just let me pay my bill." All the bar staff were silent. I wondered if the manager who would not let me use the phone had called security because I was chatting up the girls.

"Oh, you can finish your lunch, sir."

"Very kind," I said. I turned back to the bar and took a bite of some fries. I looked over my shoulder at the security guards. They had not moved from their position a couple of metres away, and they still wore those absurd grins. It was apparent that they were not going to move. The ridiculousness of it was too much.

"Can I have my bill, please?" I said.

I paid my bill and followed the security guards out of the restaurant. On my way out I saw a pair of sunglasses on the hostess station. Since no one was around, I grabbed the glasses and put them into my pocket.

Walking behind the guards, I saw they both had handcuffs attached to the back of their belts. It was all becoming hilarious. What were these two adolescents going to do with those handcuffs? Subdue a suspect and cuff him to a fence?

"I know the way to my boat," I said. "You don't have to walk with me."

"We have to walk with you and make sure you move," one kid replied.

"You must be joking," I said.

"No sir," he said. I noticed that the "sir" lacked any hint of the respect the term usually engendered.

"You know something about boats?" I said. "They have their own set of laws. For instance, once on the water, it is your own island. No one can come on board, including, and most importantly, the police. If the police wish to board a boat, they need a warrant. Interesting, no?"

"It is interesting," said the guard without turning, his shoulders hunched in a fair impression of the hunchback of Notre Dame.

I ground my teeth. By this time we had reached the boat. One of the guards turned his back on me and spoke to the attendant. I climbed on board and disappeared below. There, I grabbed my sailing knife, a wood-handled straight-blade affair sheathed in leather. I clambered back on deck, knife in hand. In full view, I pulled the knife out of the sheath horizontally, keeping the tip just inside sheath, and examined the blade. Sunlight exploded off it. I glanced up at the security guard. He faltered a half-step back — though the absurd smile did not disappear. What do I have to do, I thought, to get rid of that ridiculous smile? I sighed, popped the blade back in, and stowed the knife in the port locker.

"Thanks, guys!" I said. "Cast off the lines."

The attendant did so, and I fired the engine to life. No explosion. I engaged the throttle and powered out of the marina. Moving a little too fast in my desire to leave, I oversteered the course out the gap and had to make a large correction to make the breakwall — fishtailing the boat through the gap.

I was glad to be out of the marina, it was Bizarro-land. But my irritation at the guards' rudeness stayed with me as I snapped on my life vest and looked out on the lake. Sunlight sparkled its infinite diamonds across the water. Dozens of boats were out on the lake now, and the white triangles of sails painted a sweet scene. I turned a little at the helm to take in more of the great expanse of water — a huge police boat was steaming around the wooded headland behind me. The headland sheltered the marina entrance and the police boat was close ... *very* close.

The police boat was a large affair — twin inboard diesel engines, vastly overpowered and capable of tremendous speeds. Never a hope of outrunning her, should one even want to try. The boat was angled out into the lake, but as I watched, she snapped into a course right on my tail.

[CHAPTER THREE]

Still, if you will not fight for the right when you can easily win without bloodshed; if you will not fight when your victory will be sure and not too costly; you may come to the moment when you will have to fight with all the odds against you and only a precarious chance of survival.

— Winston Churchill, *The Gathering Storm*

"Bloody cops," I muttered. "Sure know how to wreck a day."

I wondered why they would be interested in me. I was wearing my life jacket. There were dozens of other boats out on the lake to choose from. The police were generally more interested in powerboats than sailboats, for the simple fact that you have to know what you were doing to make a sailboat move. A quick glance and I could count three stinkpots tearing about. I, meanwhile, was simply motoring slowly on a straight course.

True, I was on a boat that was not my own, but no one else knew that. The incident at the marina had happened less than two minutes ago, so it could not be that either. I surmised they were just being cops and following me because they had nothing else to do.

I steered a smooth, curving course back out into the basin. I looked back and only saw the huge bluff bow and the word POLICE emblazoned atop the cabin — they were locked on my course.

"Fuckers," I said.

After about another minute I spotted another police boat speeding in my direction, off the port bow. This one was a red twenty-foot inflatable Zodiac with what looked like something like a hundred-and-fifty-horsepower engine off the back. She had four officers in her, and they were charging over the water at an absurd speed, bouncing wildly when they hit a rogue wave. I watched in anticipation of one of the officers getting thrown from the craft, then pursed my lips as the boat settled back into a stable course, all her crew still aboard.

This is getting stupid, I thought and throttled the engine back to neutral. The Zodiac continued straight for me, her intention unmistakable. I glanced back; she had throttled back as well, and was holding station behind me. The red Zodiac slid up to within hailing distance.

"Philip Hyde?" called an officer with short blond hair, dressed, I noted, slightly different than the others.

"Yes," I said, taken aback that they knew my name.

"I'm from Emergency Medical Services, the EMS. I'm not a police officer. There is something I need to talk to you about. Can we tie up to you?"

I knew full well that as soon as I did that, they could board my vessel, search her, and take me into custody, but as long as I did not give my permission, I still had some measure of control, and I had no intention of relinquishing that control until I knew what this was about.

"No," I said, "you may not. If you have something to say, say it from there."

The officers and the EMS man exchanged looks.

"Fine," said the EMS man. "We have a report from your grandmother that you have written a suicide note."

"Ridiculous!" I said.

"Nonetheless, I must speak to you about this," replied the EMS officer, his voice distorting through the breeze.

"I am out here on a beautiful day," I said, "enjoying the weather — sailing. You think that I have written a suicide note! This is ludicrous."

"Yes, I am sure it is. May we please tie up to you and discuss it?"

The EMS man seemed calm and polite. I considered my options: I could not permit the men to moor to my boat. I could simply sit there all day long, but it was quite clear they were not going to leave. I could allow them to moor to my boat, but this would be silly since, I noted, the current and wind were slowly pushing both of us toward the rocks of the headland, to which the officers were oblivious. I decided to engender some kind of goodwill.

"All right," I said. "Let's talk about it. Let's take the boats into the harbour and tie up." I gestured to the public wall inside the breakwater, about a kilometre away, at the far end of the mooring basin I had left a few hours earlier. "I'll meet you there."

This seemed to satisfy the officers on the Zodiac. I fired up the engine and made for the wall, using that short time to figure out some form of strategy. It was all moot, though, for I was, for all intents and purposes, already surrounded.

As I passed through the breakwall, I blinked to be sure I was seeing correctly. Another huge twin-diesel police boat was threading her way through the multitude of moored boats. She looked like a large animal stalking slowly though the trees toward her prey. Her presence only served to incense me further. What in God's name did these guys think they were doing? I angled the boat toward the wall, where I saw no fewer than four police cars. Four! How many guys did they need? If I was surrounded before, what was this? Encirclement by a battalion?

I breathed deeply. Focus on getting the boat onto the wall, I told myself. I gently aligned the boat with the wall in preparation for making a sweeping turn. But my concentration was broken by a voice coming over the stern port quarter. I snapped my head around — another red Zodiac bobbed there, holding two officers. This made four boats total. The officer on the wheel was a puffy red-faced man. I was on my final approach to the breakwall, angled just right and preparing to make the large sweeping turn to glide onto the wall — a bit of a tricky manoeuvre ...

"Head for shore!" hailed a police officer.

"I am!" I shot back.

The officer, not at all far away now, adjusted the course of his Zodiac so that the bows of the two boats were on a collision course.

"Head for shore!" he said. He had a hard look that was obviously intended to intimidate.

"Hold your course!" I called, and muttered, "goddamn it."

"Head for shore!"

"Hold your course!"

It was no use. It was unheard of to put boats on a collision course, unnautical in the extreme. The boats collided. The sailboat's heavy bow compressed the Zodiac's inflatable hull and then bounced off it, slipping the sailboat a few degrees off course — ruining the smooth approach to shore.

I looked the officer, who by this time had drawn even with me, right in the eye. He was so close that I did not have to raise my voice.

"That's why you hold your course," I said.

Guilty acknowledgment flooded the officer's eyes. That was enough for me. I shook my head and swung the helm hard over, careening the boat in a tight turn, switching the throttle to neutral as I did so — allowing the turn to dissipate the boat's speed. As I drew even with the wall, my course was still off. A few metres of water sat between the boat and wall. A marine police office stood in wait.

"Toss me your line," he said.

"I'm too far off the wall."

"Don't worry, I'll pull you in."

I considered it for a moment. The officer must have noticed my hesitation. He stood with his feet apart and raised his arms in a T. This was a seldom-used manoeuvre simply because it made a person look a little silly. I was impressed that the officer employed the move. I grabbed the line and tossed it at him. It hit him in the arm, and he grabbed it and hauled the boat in.

"Nice docking," the officer said when he had finished securing the boat.

"Thanks — not an easy thing to do alone."

I considered saying something about the yahoo who had collided with me, but as I looked about, the words dropped from my mind. Four police cruisers still stood at the curb, two officers to a car. Two large police boats lay bobbing on the wall, with crews of four. Two Zodiacs were being secured to the wall, four officers in one and two in the other. All told, there were over twenty police officers present.

I felt my adrenaline surge, and flexed my arms in effort to keep it under control. I could feel my thinking begin to become clouded and unreliable: one second I was counting cops, the next counting guns, and a black rage carried me into completely unreasonable and unhelpful places. I attempted to bring my mind under control. In a way, I reasoned, it was somewhat flattering, twenty-plus police to one. Then my mind shot away from me: What the fuck are they all doing here? With this thought my adrenaline shot through the roof, pumping into my muscles, dilating my pupils, sending my thoughts skipping away. I breathed again, deeply, and struggled to bring myself under control.

I stepped off the boat and found myself flanked by two officers. They were not close — five or six steps off — but it was clear that I was not going anywhere. None of the officers looked at me, which I found to be an interesting fact. After a few beats, a tall blond officer, his muscular build straining his uniform, slipped through the flanking officers. The chevrons on his arms denoted him the sergeant in charge. Trailing him was the EMS man.

I suddenly understood why the officers flanking me were not making eye contact and not speaking. They were waiting for the EMS. They all were under the impression that I had written a suicide note. It was preposterous.

I looked over the sergeant. I noted his black side arm. It was almost camouflaged against his black belt and navy uniform. In the centre of his belt was another holster. The barrel of a taser peaked out striped yellow and black, like a wasp. The obvious simile intended by the designers was offensive. The sting of a taser was nothing like the sting of a wasp. There had been much in the news lately about officers using tasers to subdue suspects. Tasers were supposed to be harmless, but people were dying. Officers seemed far more inclined to use these weapons than they were a firearm. A taser did not hold the same gravity as a firearm, or even as much gravity as physical restraint. This knowledge only served to heighten my agitation, and images of thousands of volts of electricity flowing through my body, very much like the arcane electroshock therapy, flooded my mind. Knowing that I'd been diagnosed with bipolar disorder, and that the electricity could potentially do me some serious harm, that taser frightened me deeply. I was also acutely aware that I was in a hyperagitated state in a tense situation. Just the type of situation where people got tasered.

Worst of all, I was not sure I could hold my temper. I felt it growing, swelling, churning below the surface. The tide might crash over the shore of my consciousness at any moment.

I looked back at the EMS officer. He was of slim build and looked very calm. It appeared that this was his show.

"I think I'll sit down," I said.

"Good idea," replied the EMS officer as I sat on a small ledge by the water.

"Here's what's happening," he said, crouching in front of me. "We got a call that you had written a suicide note. Your grandmother called your uncle, and he called us. When we get a call like this, we have to take you to the hospital to be examined by a doctor."

"Let me see if I get this straight," I said, shaking my head. "My grandmother, who I don't live with, and who is ninety-two, by the way — and who, I would add, needs a magnifying glass to read — says I wrote a suicide note."

"That's correct."

"And you need all these guys to take care of this," I said, sweeping my hand toward the other officers.

"I guess there is not too much else happening," said the EMS officer with a shrug. I nodded, and felt my adrenaline key back a notch. This guy was good.

"We have to take you to the hospital," he said.

"What if I refuse? As you can see, there is nothing wrong. I've been sailing — sailing — and you are really ruining my day."

"These guys have to take you the hospital." He gestured with his head to the officer standing behind him. He said it in such a way that made me think he did not believe them to be the brightest bulbs in the box.

I glanced away from the EMS officer to look the police sergeant, the only other person looking at me, in the eyes. I saw no malice there. With effort, I breathed deeply: inhaling positive energy, exhaling negative. I stepped outside myself, saw no alternative, observed the emotions raging with me, and switched gears.

"Okay," I said. "Let's go."

"Excellent," said the EMS officer, slapping me on the leg. "These guys would not have left here without you."

I rose to my feet slowly, centred. I felt like the EMS officer and I were in the eye of a hurricane, while the rest of the world swirled around. I wanted to say that when this was all over I'd buy him a drink, but I reconsidered, thinking it might be inappropriate. Instead I said, "When all this is over I'll buy you a tea."

A smile spread across the EMS officer's face. "Excellent." He turned to the sergeant. "Let's get Philip to the car," he said.   He gestured for me to walk to the nearest cruiser.

I took one step and felt rage punch through the calm like an automobile thrown into the eye of that hurricane. In a voice originating from my belly, I bellowed:

"I want you — all — to know: I am a Canadian citizen."

My voice echoed and rattled around the harbour, and twenty pairs of eyes swivelled in their sockets. It was as though everything within hearing — the officers, the birds, the waves — paused to listen to my words. I looked into at least ten of those pairs of eyes, and none that I could see bore any rancour.

"Smartly done," said the sergeant in a voice only I could hear and without turning his head.

Together we walked to the nearest squad car, my posture Marine straight. I was approached by an officer of medium height with curly black hair, who appeared to take control.

"We have to search you, sir. Part of procedure, I'm afraid," he said.

"Fine, let's get this over with."

The officer took out some cash, a wallet, a pack of cigarettes, and a pen from my pockets while I pressed my hands onto the warm metal of the squad car roof.

"Your going to need this," said the officer, handing it all back to me. "Since you have been so cooperative, we are not going to cuff you. And ... you get to ride with the girls." He gestured over to a squad car where two dirty-blonde female officers stood.

I guess it's not all bad, I thought, but managed not to say anything. One of the female officers opened the rear door for me and I climbed in.

Unfortunately, this was not my first time riding in the back of a squad car. It was stuffy, the air thick, due to the car having been sitting in the summer sun, and there was absolutely no leg room. The ladies piled into the cruiser and we pulled away from the water. I noted that these officers were quite young, and could not have been on the force for very long. I couldn't help myself ...

"Not very much leg room in these things."

"No, I suppose not," said the driver.

"You must see some interesting things driving around in this car all day."

"We see a lot of different things. We tend to see extremes, very good along with very bad."

"I could imagine," I said.

The hospital was not very far away, and as I chatted with the officers I wondered vaguely why I was so talkative and why I was not still seething with anger. It did not quite fit. I knew that one of the symptoms of the illness I was accused of having was that one can become overtly sexual — unsafe sexual practices, they said — and a voice told me there might be something wrong with sitting in the back of a squad car flirting with the officers in the front. Aside from that, flirting with a woman with a side arm, any woman, was probably not a good idea either. What if you said the wrong thing? I also wondered, below that train of thought, if the police had put me in that car on purpose, to keep me calm.

Not enjoying these lines of reasoning, I kept chatting with the women. We pulled up to the emergency entrance and parked right in front.

"Star parking, ladies," I said.

An enormous woman, wearing a bulletproof vest, walked out the hospital door with an orderly. She carried a soda and a chocolate bar. A smear of chocolate clung to the corner of her mouth.

"If I have to deal with one more loony tune today, I'm going to lose it," she said to her companion, her voice grating and whiny. As she drew even with us, she turned her gaze on me. Her eyes were hard black stones, void of compassion. A shiver ran down my spine. She was so fat, her vest looked like a tea towel shoved into her blouse for dinner. If you shot at her, fifty percent of her torso would be an uncovered target. As she walked by I read the word NURSE printed on the back of the vest.

Nice, I thought. A nurse so clearly ill herself.

We walked into the hospital and stood in line at the triage station: a man with a bandage over his eye, an old man in a wheelchair, a mother with a baby cradled in her arm, and me, flanked by two female police officers. I chatted jovially.

"I hate waiting in these lines. Always takes forever," I said. I shifted my weight from foot to foot as I spoke.

As we approached the triage station I said, "Please remember to tell the attendant that I am here on a voluntary basis."

"Sure thing," said an officer.

Our turn came, and I checked in.

[Chapter Four]

When they are at Rome, they do there as they see done.
— Robert Burton, *Anatomy of Melancholy*

We walked down a wide corridor. The officers seemed to know where they were going. Eventually, we came to a sign hanging from the ceiling, reading "Mental Health Emergency," pointed down a narrow dead-end corridor. Quiet now, I stepped down the hallway. We came to a massive steel door, its purpose unmistakable: it was designed to keep people in. Beside the door was a buzzer that read "Press for entry," and above the door was a security camera, in a protective plastic covering. I felt my emotions slip into a red-hot rage.

I turned to one of the officers. "I'm not going in there," I said.

"You have to," she said, her eyes remaining light.

"Maybe you are not understanding me," I said. "Under no circumstances am I going to walk through that door. If you want me to enter that door, you are going to have to arrest me."

In an instant, the officer's eyes switched to a state of professional stoicism, and I regretted giving her the idea.

"Fine, turn around," she said, pulling cuffs from her belt.

For the second time that day, adrenaline surged into my muscular system. I knew that this was more a protest than anything else. I knew also I would have to go into that room. But there was no way I was going to walk in voluntarily.

I turned, and the nice lady I'd been flirting with snapped cuffs onto my wrists. Not too tight — she just snapped them on — but I flexed my wrists so the cuffs cut into my flesh. The physical pain seemed to reinforce the injustice I felt. The officer punched the buzzer and the lock sprang open. Evidently, someone had been watching. The officer pulled open the door and ushered me in.

An appalling sight greeted me. I stood rail straight, cuffs cutting into my wrists behind my back.

The room was essentially a square. Off to the right were three beds, occupied by haggard, disturbed-looking people wrapped in thin sheets. They all looked dazed, their gazes rolling haphazardly around the ceiling.

The left corner was glassed off and contained the nurses' station. The half dozen people inside the station seemed not to pay me much attention. Apparently, a cuffed man being ushered into the room by two female police officers was not an unusual occurrence.

The remaining areas of the room sported overstuffed vinyl couches and armchairs. A melange of people paced around the room or sat, idly, in the armchairs. I was sure I too would be spending some time in these.

Three frosted windows over the beds admitted little light. The floors were filthy, and pads of dust had taken up residence in the corners. I was not sure what type of hospital permitted dirt to collect on the floors, but I was sure that it was not one I would wish to be in.

An officer snapped the cuffs off my wrists one at a time. I examined the deep red bands around each wrist. I turned to face one of the officers, and she looked back at me, doe-eyed. But rage had me now and I wished to wound her in some way. I brought my wrist into her field of view and watched. I saw a flicker of distress in her expression, and to bring the point home I said, "Look at this."

"Wait here," she said, again switching on the stoicism, and turned to the glassed-in nurses' station. She said a few words to a nurse and, without looking back, the officers left. I was left standing alone in the middle of the room with my proverbial finger up my ass.

Not seeing much alternative, I sat in one of the overstuffed plastic armchairs. It squeaked sterilely under my weight.

Taking in the room again, I thought one could easily describe it as a small jail. Guards dressed in black milled about in the back of the nurses' station. No one appeared much to care for the wretched-looking people in their charge. I knew better, though. I knew that it was just a room. I knew that it was just in a hospital. I knew that the real wretched were those behind the glass. *Those* were the institutionalized — those who paid lip service to care but who were void of compassion. I pitied them.

I blew out a steady stream of air and considered my options. I knew I could be kept here until I saw a doctor.

Escape? Impossible without some form of violence, and why was I thinking that, anyway? I only had to speak to a doctor and clear this up. Besides, the door was on a buzzer system monitored by video. I noticed that whenever someone wandered close to the door, the seemingly uninterested people behind the glass shed their veils of disinterest.

Worst case, the doctor could put me on a form, suspending my civil rights for three days, keeping me at the hospital against my will. Again, a thin layer of my mind wondered why I was even considering escape. I was only here to meet a doctor, no? Was it the rage? With little else to do, I sat and reflected on the uselessness of that particular emotion.

I heard someone call my name and turned to look at a middle-aged blonde woman adorned with what I would politely call creative jewellery. I followed her down a short hallway, where she unlocked a heavy door. I looked at the steel monstrosity as I walked into the room and wondered if it would kill them to put a little thought into aesthetics. The room was small, furnished with a plastic-covered couch and a chair.

"Nice," I said. "Who's your decorator?" The woman gestured for me to sit on the couch while she took the chair facing me.

"I'm Riva, the intake nurse," she said in a heavy Polish accent.

Nodding, I quickly accessed my strategy: I must not talk too much, and I must not talk too fast. These were symptoms of a manic phase of bipolar disorder and grounds to keep me.

If they thought I had written a suicide note, they would be looking for any reason to keep me. It was possible that this was all a mistake, and I must do my best to explain that to them.

"Why don't you tell me why you are here," Riva said.

I began to recount the story of the boat, the police officers, and the alleged note. But something happened — I was talking fast, at an outrageous clip, and my mouth began to feel pasty. Once I started, on and on the words came, like tumbleweed blown about the desert. When I finally noticed, I groped about for a way to cover my tracks.

"I know I am talking fast and quite a lot, but I've had a trying day. I want to assure you that I did not write that note — I was out sailing, having a fine day, when all this happened. This is ludicrous. You understand, of course."

"All right," said Riva, stretching her neck. "Why don't you go and wait outside. Procedure dictates that we have to get an on-call physician and the on-call psychiatrist to look over you."

I examined her closely: she seemed genuine. I was miffed that I had wasted so much time on the first-level staff. It was a bit like going into a clothing store — you never want the person who greets you at the door to help you. They are generally the rookies, placed there on welcoming duty by the senior staff.

"Fine," I said, and walked out of the room back to the squeaky armchair.

* * *

After what seemed like an unusually long period of time, a man in surgical scrubs breezed into the room. He was about six feet tall with close-cropped, well-maintained hair. He must have got it trimmed every two weeks. He was, evidently, from his self-assigned importance, the emergency room doctor. He barely looked around, instead focusing on the clipboard in his hand and standing in the middle of the room.

"Philip," he said, looking at the clipboard.

I shook my head and stirred myself from the chair to join the doctor in the middle of the room: an informal conference, then. He looked up briefly, then back at the clipboard.

"I'm Dr. Avial. What happened?"

Disturbed that the doctor was not looking me in the eye, I attempted to stay even keeled.

"There was a mistake," I said. "If you can believe it, my grandmother believed she discovered a suicide note, written by me. She called my uncle, who reported it to the police. I was out sailing and the police brought me here."

Still not looking at me, the doctor ticked something off on his clipboard and signed the bottom.

"I see," he said. "That's it for now." He turned on his heel and walked back through the nurses' station, paused to speak to a nurse, their heads bowed, and disappeared through the back door.

I was, again, left standing in the middle of the room feeling I really should stick my thumb up my ass, for it would be more productive. There, people milling about me, I began to suspect the truth of my situation. They intended to keep me here. They

— the state, my uncle — intended to suspend my rights and keep me locked in this room. There had been no call from my grandmother. My uncle, a clever lawyer — I had to give him that — had manipulated the state, the police, into finding me, taking me into custody, and bringing me here. One almost had to admire the diabolical nature of the plan. But as the pieces fell together, a tempest slammed into my body and clouded my thoughts. The muscles in my arms began to tense and my jaw clenched. I strode to the window of the nurses' station.

"Ah, Philip, good," said the nurse seated on the other side. "You have been put on a Form 3. Do you know what this is?"

Momentarily taken aback I said, "I certainly do. But how is this possible? I only spoke to the doctor for less than a minute. How can he render a diagnosis in that time? Also, I have not spoken to a *psychiatrist*."

The nurse shrugged and handed me a copy of a form. In the top left corner was emblazoned the crest of the Ontario government, and the sheet was titled "FORM 3." It was signed at the bottom. She also handed me a pamphlet entitled "Your Rights."

"A rights adviser will come visit you within twelve hours," she added. I had met some of the rights advisers in the past and knew of their uselessness.

"I demand to have this form reviewed," I said.

"There is nothing to be done," she said. "Once the form is signed, it cannot be rescinded for the duration of the form. There is a phone behind you that you may use."

With that, the nurse closed the window in my face and shuffled to the back of the station. I considered banging on the glass with my fist, but instead I strode over to the phone and dialled my uncle's mobile number.

"Hello," came the voice of my uncle.

"Are you happy?" I said.

"Happy's got nothing to do with it."

For a moment I allowed that it may be true, that my grandmother, being in her nineties, had become confused and alerted him.

"You know Grandmother is ninety-two," I said, "and for Christ's sake, can't even read without a magnifying glass."

"That might be so, but she was quite confident."

"They have put me on a Form 3, I can't do anything. Get down here and do something about it."

"I can't do that."

I had been enraged before, but the last vestige of calm disappeared at those words. It felt as though someone had ignited the hem of my pants and I was becoming enveloped in white flames of anger.

"Listen to me, you motherfucker. You and I both know there was no suicide note. I am going to do everything I can to get you disbarred for this. I am going to go to the Law Society. I'm going to wherever I have to. I am going to make your life a living motherfucking hell."

My uncle's voice seemed to shrink. "I am sorry you are so angry with me."

"Fuck you," I said and slammed down the phone.

"Hey," said a nurse. She was leaning through the window of the nurses' station. "Keep it down, and easy on the phone."

"Piss off," I said. "You're not the one locked up in here."

She shrugged, apparently satisfied this constituted a legitimate explanation, and slid the glass closed.

After a time of staring at the phone on the wall, I repaired to one of the armchairs. I sat in that chair for a long time, considering my options. I knew people, through work I had done, through my family. Connections that I did not often call upon.

I got up and walked over to the phone and dialled a number. Reaching a receptionist, I asked for William. William owned a forensics firm specializing in dealing with engineering issues, the firm I worked at before I'd taken some time off. Whenever I'd described my job to people, they inevitably said, "Oh, like *CSI*." My response to that was "Yes, minus the neon blue, blood-detector light."

Due to the nature of his work, William was often in court, presenting his findings as evidence. Accordingly, he knew many a lawyer.

"How you doing, Philip?" William said.

"Not too good, to tell you the truth. I've got to cut to the chase."

"Shoot," he said.

"My grandmother thought I wrote a suicide note, which I did not. She told my uncle, who called the police. The police found me, took me to the hospital, they have put me on a Form 3, suspending my rights, and intend to keep me here for at least three days. Can you help me? I need a lawyer." I could always communicate directly with William if I had to — no layering in emotion, just simple facts.

"I see," William said. "Give me five minutes and call me back."

I clicked off, waited five minutes exactly. Good to have engineers around from time to time, I reflected. When they say five minutes, they mean five minutes. I rang William back up.

"Well?" I said.

William was probably thirty years my senior, but I still considered him a friend of equal footing. He was a grey-haired Irishman, a former olympic wrestler, from a large family, never married, and liked younger woman. I had suffered through many a story of how he had dated some girl then broke it off when she tried to move his furniture around.

"Are you all right?" he said. "Are you sure this —"

My anger flashed, and just as quickly I got it under control. I was on a hair trigger.

"Are you going to help me or not? I've got to know."

"I'll be right there," said William. "Sit tight."

"All right," I said and rang off.

I went back and sat in my squeaky chair. Sitting there, I was confident that William would come by and we would design a strategy. Nothing to do but wait.

There was a small part of me that, had I been able to look at it, would have wondered why I was really here. My uncle would not have undertaken this course lightly. That small part of myself would have thought, Perhaps I am ill; perhaps it is good that I am here. But because I was being forced to look — I would not, I would never. So I sat and waited for William and the lawyer.

Presently, and faster than I expected, the big steel door swung open and William strode in. He was a big guy and still in good shape. He was carrying a couple of plastic bags. After him was his mother. Somewhere in her late seventies and mother of seven, she wore thick glasses that obfuscated her sharp eyes. She was tough as a fighting nun and sweet as the green grass of the Emerald Isles from which she hailed. I could not resist a small smile. Some lawyer.

The two pulled up vinyl armchairs. The chairs' large arms made it difficult to bring them close together, so they turned them slightly, making a rough semicircle. Mrs. Carthaigh sat down, placing her handbag in her lap.

"Are you all right, laddie?" she asked.

The question was so absurd that all I could do was shake my head and chuckle.

"Yes, I'm fine," I said.

"That's what I thought," she said, patting my thigh, and I could have sworn her smile conveyed some secret knowledge.

While we had been talking, William had been standing over us, pulling rectangular cardboard boxes from the bags. They looked like Chinese food cartons, but far more elegant, like something you might wrap a present in.

"We brought you something to eat," said William, handing the cartons over one at a time. They smelled of the divine, spicy and sweet-orange at the same time.

"Duck wings," he said.

My eyes widened.

He paused. "I hope you like duck," he added.

"I certainly do," I said. William relaxed.

There were three containers. The first held a light spring salad. The second, duck wings lightly glazed with a delicious-looking golden sauce, and the third, what looked like mini pan-fired potato latkes.

"Tuck in," said William. I realized I was famished. I breathed deeply, resolving to enjoy the food, and grabbed a wing. It was delicious, savoury and sweet and tenderly cooked. Next, I had some of the salad, and became aware that Mrs. Carthaigh and William were watching me with satisfaction. It occurred to me that perhaps I should say something about the situation. I opened my mouth to speak, but in the calmness that part of myself that knew I should be here surged to the surface. I felt large tears begin to leak from my eyes. I was, I realized, under enormous stress. I decided to let them roll, in the hope of relieving some of that pressure, for I had read that tears contain cortisol, a hormone whose release helps relieve stress.

Again thinking that I should say something, I opened my mouth, only to be interrupted by William.

"Eat your food," he said.

I nodded and ate the exquisite meal from the beautiful cardboard boxes, making no effort to wipe the tears from my face.

* * *

After the food and the tears, I felt more centred, more balanced. Not much was spoken between the three of us. Nothing about a lawyer, just an "Are you going to be okay?" from William.

"I'll be fine," I replied.

"Take care of yourself," William said.

"Aye, Philip, take care," said Mrs Carthaigh. With looks of reassurance, they left.

I sat in my vinyl throne for a long time after that, tired and empty. There was nothing else to do. No television, no books, no magazines. The others in that dirty, fluorescent-lit room were not people I particularly wanted to talk to. I was sure they would not help my cause much, at best only add confusion. A woman in the corner had hospital sheets wrapped around her body and a towel wrapped around her head. She mumbled scripture with a bowed head. An African man lay on one of the vinyl hospital beds with his head in the lap of a girl who must have been his visiting girlfriend. She looked apprehensive but resolute as she stroked his hair and assured him that everything would be all right.

Others in the three hospital beds across the room looked to be somewhat comatose, entwined in white hospital sheets. I could not help but feel pity, sadness, at the depth of their plight. Those behind the glass studiously avoided me. There was nothing to do but wait. So wait I did. Hours passed. What little natural light there was managed to eek in through the frosted glass windows covered by thick, cross-hatched metal screening. A digital clock above the windows blazed out the "o'clock" in red numbers. But for some reason, perhaps because there was nothing to associate this reading with, the clock did little to mark time's passage. I would look up and four minutes had passed. After what I thought was another four minutes had passed, I would look up and two hours would have gone.

At some point in the hours after William and his mother left, I resolved to simply get through these next days. I would say as little as possible, not cause a scene, keep my temper under control. I reflected on my experiences and on the vacillation of my emotions since the morning. It was of little consequence. What was required now was equanimity and calmness. The state had suspended my civil rights for three days, and I was sure they wanted nothing more than to suspend them further. At this point, I was under observation. It was all conjecture at this point: the suicide note, even the fact that I had been diagnosed with a bipolar disorder. I would not have anyone touch me, force assistance upon me. If I required help, that would be my choice. Though they could keep me here, they could not force me to take anything. A court order was required for that. They would probably try to *trick* me into taking something. Again I felt my anger rise.

Calmness, that is what is required. I breathed to myself — I would get through this seventy-two hour form, and then those who were responsible would pay.

That part of myself that had welled to the surface in realization that perhaps I should be here evaporated, replaced by resolve.

This tactic of calmness was to be put to the test. In the early evening, a pleasant, slightly paunchy Indian nurse emerged from behind the glass.

"How are you, Philip?" she asked.

I raised my eyebrows but said nothing.

She nodded in a kindly way and said, "I understand. I have to take a sample of your blood."

"You must be joking," I said.

"Why would I be? We need to see if there are any substances in your blood — if there is any medication, and in what concentrations. It's standard procedure."

"Under no circumstances," I replied, my eyes narrowing, "will I allow you to take a sample of my blood."

The nurse retreated behind the glass. The gall of these people, I thought. They can keep me here, but they cannot have my blood. I watched the nurse in conversation with a tall, male, black nurse wearing white scrubs. Nice colour, I thought. The man looked at me and walked out from behind the glass. He crouched by my chair. His brown eyes held a gentle look in them.

"Philip, we need to take a sample of your blood."

As I had watched the two nurses speak, I had felt my ire rise, but now I looked the nurse straight in the eyes and said, "Again, under no circumstances will I permit you to take a sample of my blood."

"In that case we will have to call Security."

"Call them and see what happens. I'm so angry at what is happening here, I wouldn't mind kicking the crap out of a few guys."

The gentle look did not falter from the man's eyes. In fact, it seemed to deepen.

"They will just call more guys," he said. "All we need is a small sample, it is our policy — we have your concerns at heart."

I had a vision of fourteen security guards in black uniforms all standing around me waiting for something to happen. The police arriving, hands on their side arms. The situation would spiral so far out of control, I would have to agree, and they would get their blood sample. And with it, a lot of trouble, and in the end, another reason to keep me here.

With my martial training, I knew I could engage two guards if I wanted to, do some damage on four, but any more than that was a lost cause. Further, I was in a locked room. There was nowhere to go. Besides, and most importantly, I had no desire to hurt anyone. I was sure they had a room nearby stocked to the brim with security guards. I realized I would love to pound a few of them, but it was not my way, and my resolve — calmness — what of that? Exhaling, I breathed out the tension in my rigid muscles.

"Okay," I said. "Let's get it done."

"Good, good," said the nurse, patting my arm. He gestured to the Indian nurse to bring out the sampling equipment. The decision made, I was equitable. With a practised hand, she placed a needle into my arm and withdrew two vials of blood. I chatted with her and the other nurse. Not for the first time that day I wondered how I could go from anger to magnanimity, even cordiality, in the span of a few moments.

The nurses left without further incident, retreating behind their glass partition. The black guy and the Indian nurse began chatting with two others. I, needing to use the restroom, got up. My route took me past an opening in the glass. I caught a snatch of the conversation. The guy seemed to be being congratulated.

"Good work," one nurse said.

"The white knight," another said.

I could not believe my ears. As the man shrugged in a fair impression of modesty, he was taking credit for my decision to remain calm. It saddened me to see this. As I walked by I caught the man's eye. The look of pride vanished.

It was all beginning to be too much. I felt suddenly very tired. I was loath to sleep in these dirty surroundings, unconscious with a group of people who could, quite reasonably, be expected to accost me in my sleeping state. I reminded myself that it was just a room in a hospital, staffed with people who were — in principle, at least — supposed to look out for me. I returned from the restroom and gathered some blankets and sheets from the linen cart. I laid a sheet on one of the vinyl beds in the corner. In all my clothes, I wrapped myself in the blankets and fell deeply asleep.

* * *

I awoke, and in a flash, the events of the previous day flooded back. The blankets I had wrapped around myself were twisted around me, and my shirt back was soaked through with sweat. I felt like I was trapped in a freakish predator vine that was slowly choking the air out of my lungs. Shaking off the image, I unwrapped the blankets from around myself and perched on the edge of the bed. I reminded myself I was at war.

First things first. I needed a shower, for as the proverb goes, cleanliness is next to godliness. I had already been to the washroom once and knew the showers were as filthy as the rest of the unit. What was it about the mentally unwell (of which I was quite sure I was not one) that those in charge of their care permitted such conditions? I was quite sure that the showers in the cardiology wing were not covered with mildew. This was not going to be fun.

On my way to the shower, a black female nurse, who obviously fancied herself a hard one, stopped me.

"We need a urine sample," she said, holding out a beaker.

I looked at her and shook my head. Bitch. I took the beaker without a word, grabbed a stack of towels from the linen rack, and closeted myself in the shower room.

I laid fresh white towels over the small, dark orange tiles in the single shower stall, leaving only the drain open. I would not allow those behind the glass partition to deprive me of such a basic habit as good hygiene. Standing on the towels, I thoroughly showered, washing my body and hair. I was starting to feel pretty good. I dried myself, wrapped a towel around my waist, and stepped out of the shower onto more towels I had laid out on the floor. Then I sat on the floor in the Japanese manner — on my knees, feet pointed straight back, neck, back, head erect. Closing my eyes, I pictured myself in an ancient Japanese room enclosed only by white, opaque, square screens. In ancient Japan, privacy was achieved not by a wall but by consciously not hearing. I pictured that everything outside this room did not exist. There was no sound, no one outside the screens. I breathed deeply and calmly, evenly exhaled. Three breaths, I thought. As I breathed, I thought — I am breathing in; I am breathing out. My mind was empty except for these words and the sensation of my breath.

As I neared the end of my third breath, words from my study of aikido flooded my mind: "When you are under attack, the whole universe is your enemy." Had I been able to digest this thought and ponder it, I would have seen the problems that it contained, but I was not able to. With that thought, I opened my eyes and breathed once more. Kneeling on those startlingly white towels, I felt centred, present with the current situation, but with space around it, space to think. I understood now. No one was to be trusted; everyone must be fought — stranger, friend, it made no difference. I was at war and I must win. These thoughts consumed me. What the war was, for whom I was fighting, I did not know, nor could I stop to consider it.

I stood and caught sight of the beaker the nurse had given me. I stood over the toilet, unscrewed the orange cap, and urinated into the jar, filling it about a quarter full. Then I moved over to the sink and filled it to the halfway mark with water. Screwing the lid, I gave it a little shake. It was a straw-yellow colour now, the appearance of the urine from a well-hydrated person. It would suffice, I thought — throwing off any test of concentration. Feeling clean and balanced, I dressed and collected the towels. Outside the bathroom, I disposed of the towels in the laundry and walked toward the glass partition. The nurse with attitude had me on her radar, and tracked me as I approached. I handed her the beaker.

"You have a good day now," I said.

* * *

For the next forty-eight hours I sat on my vinyl throne. I said little. I ate the globules of food that were set before me. Others tried to speak to me, but I replied curtly. The light in the room was eerily consistent; even at night it diffused into the room. At night I declined the vinyl bed, instead wrapping blankets around myself and sleeping in small snatches, stringing these beads of unconsciousness together through the night. I was always on guard, always watching. At one point a nurse informed me that some medication had been recommended for me. I replied that they could suspend my Charter rights with the stroke of a pen, but if they wished me to take medication, they would require a court order. That stopped them cold. Forty-eight hours and countless small containers of juice later (to keep myself alert, for I was not permitted coffee), I stood at the big steel door. My wallet and cigarettes were returned to me, and the door buzzed. Without a look back, I pulled open the door, walked outside the hospital, and lit a cigarette. Someone was going to pay, I thought, inhaling thick grey smoke and cool morning air.

I could not know that the sleeplessness, the rage, and the continual state of alertness were spinning me to a place beyond the limits of control.

This was not his first time at this hospital. As Philip turned his back on it, he felt the building loom behind him, and thoughts of his first time there flooded his mind. He had been there when depression racked his body. In the months before he had gone to the MBCT clinic, the depression had pulled at him without mercy. His mind was consumed with negative thoughts, the darkest of thoughts. He lost weight. Even the smallest of tasks was a pain-filled experience: going to the corner store, buying bus tokens, going to the bank. These small events that contained the smallest of variables were as difficult as hiking barefoot over the razored rock of an ancient lava flow.

Worse was the anxiety, as if dealing with negative thoughts was not enough. From the moment of waking until, at night, his exhausted body could no longer stay awake, he was plagued by anxiety. It was as though a dark man followed him with a loaded gun, cocked and ready, pointed at his head, at any moment prepared to pull the trigger. It was a special kind of hell, a mind filled with negative thoughts he could not switch off, clipped on the heels by the rabid dogs of anxiety.

Daily, for months on end, he would deal with these circumstances. It seemed as though there was no end, and he could not see through it.

So one day he went to his uncle's gun cabinet, squirrelled away in a back room. He extracted a high-power bear rifle, short barrel that accepted shells more suited to an anti-aircraft gun than a rifle. The rifle was matte silver and shone with deadly purpose. He wrapped the rifle in a blanket, grabbled his uncle's car keys, and headed north.

Arriving two hours later at his family's small cabin on the outskirts of Algonquin Park, he parked the car and sat on the front stoop of the old log cabin. The walls had been erected by his grandfather around 1950, built with wood from the land. A stacked pile of firewood pleasantly ate up the morning sun. Philip unwrapped the blanket, took a shell, and placed it in the chamber. But the more he tried to chamber the round, fist clamped around the bolt arm, the rough non-slip texture pulling against his skin, the more his mind rebelled. He pushed, and his mind pushed back, hard. Twice as hard his *mind pushed back, four times as hard, then ten times as hard, and he pushed back a hundred times as hard. It was like an asymptotic graph, never reaching the zero point: the closer to the zero of pressing the shell home, the more force was required — a curve shooting to infinity. As he pressed, he heard the birds sing their sweet song. He felt the pine-scented breeze on his cheek. He wanted to experience it again, he realized. He wanted to feel that breeze. He wanted to drink a cool drink, to sail a boat into the teeth of the wind, to feel a woman's soft bosom on his cheek, to taste the sweet scent of the summer air.*

A smiled pulled at the corners of his mouth. He laid the rifle down and extracted the shell. He rolled it up in the blanket and placed the deadly package back in the trunk.

"Steel yourself," he said, looking round at the tall evergreens that stood over him, his friends.

He drove back to Toronto, replaced the firearm, and walked to the hospital emergency room. There they told him of the MBCT program. He had his psychiatrist refer him, and somehow she expedited the process. Within a week he began the program. After its conclusion, he came back to the hospital daily, to sit in groups, to consult with the doctor to find a medication to lift him from his depression. After the groups, he enrolled in another Mindfulness program at the hospital. Eventually he learned to slip off his dark thoughts. Over and over he did this. Without considering those thoughts' nature, he just unlocked from them and let them recede. He learned to use his anxiety, breathing with it, allowing it to flow through him. Three breaths. Breathing: I know that I am breathing in. Breathing: I know that I am breathing out. Breathing, he would feel the power of anxiety in his body, know that it was there. In that seeing of it, in that observation, there was a type of space. It caused him to be able to view it with abstraction; it defused the negativity. Then he could use its power, its energy, for his own purpose. Anxiety has terrific power, he learned. It causes the muscles to become fantastically strong. Think of the middle-aged woman who lifted a city bus that had trapped her child. It speeds cognition, allow one to solve problems faster. It dilates the pupils to allow more light into the eye, to see more. It speeds the transmission of signals along the nervous system. In removing the negativity of anxiety, its power to control his mind, he was able to channel it, get on top of it, surf it, so that he could use it.

There was no mistaking that going to the hospital and dealing with this issue had been a great challenge. And though he recognized his triumph, negative memories often plagued him. As he strode away from the hospital, he bitterly cursed those who had forced those experiences back into his mind, and swore to bring the tenor of that pain to their door.

The fire of my temper burned hot, and as I strode down the street, my thoughts jumped and skidded like water tossed into a hot skillet of oil. I pulled up short on the walk. Would it not be better, I wondered, to balm my mind before I considered what to do next? Unwilling to go home, near broke, and at odds with my family — unarguably, a difficult situation to get under control. I felt ire rise again as I thought of those responsible for my plight.

I ducked off the road to the nearest pay phone, located Heather's card in my wallet, and rang up her mobile.

"Hello," her honey-laced voice answered. I could tell by the background noise that she was in her car, probably driving home from work.

"Three guesses as to who this is, as long as the first guess is Philip," I said.

"What ever happened to sailing, sailor?" she tittered.

"Long story, actually. The weather turned stormy," I said. "I wonder if I could cash in that proverbial rain check? It's Friday, after work — pretty good time for a drink. Would you be interested ... I mean, would you like ... How about going for a drink?" I silently cursed my conversational breakdown. Real smooth.

"What would you like to do after that drink?" she asked.

"Long walk on the beach?"

"You know what? I'll do you one better," she laughed. "I'm going up to my cottage in Temagami. I was planning on going up alone, but if you're free this weekend, why don't you come up with me?"

This seemed too good to be true. A weekend out of the hurtling masses of Toronto would be just the ticket. A thought of her naked breast and golden hair shining in the northern sun stirred me.

"I would love to," I said. "I mean it, but I am having some difficulties."

"Hold on, I'm pulling over."

I lit a cigarette and waited.

"What's going on, Philip?" she asked.

I thought for a moment, thought of our first conversation, and in a moment of lucidity I decided again for honesty.

"I've just been to the hospital, I've been there for a few days. I am ... going through something."

"What are you going through?" she asked, her voice soft, the embodiment of femininity.

"I'd rather not say," I said, feeling the quaking of strong emotion in my throat. "I like you, I do, I remember our first conversation, more than the other stuff ... though I remember *that* well, too."

A gurgle of laughter rolled through the hard receiver pressed against my ear.

"I want to give us a chance," I continued, "and what I'm dealing with is too much. I have to deal with it on my own. If you get involved, I don't know how to deal with it ... and it ... it would not be good for you."

"Philip, let me help you," she said. "Tell me what's wrong."

"You must understand."

"Philip, please, tell me the problem, I'm sure —"

I hung up the phone.

[CHAPTER FIVE]

Who said you should call a spade a spade?

— Anonymous

I crushed my cigarette out under my foot, turned, and headed for the streetcar. Twenty minutes later I was standing at the gates to the yacht club. I punched the code into the pedestrian entrance. The lock clicked, and I swung open the heavy gate and entered the club. The club grounds were essentially a large parking lot, with the clubhouse sitting on the western edge next to the water. The building was sided in whitewashed wood, and looked more like a plantation mansion than a yacht club. Why someone would commission a clubhouse of this design for a sailing club was beyond me.

Striding through the lot, I looked neither left nor right. I was not sure where I was going to go, but I had to get away. I would get my boat in the water, sail for a few hours, and drop anchor.

I walked around the clubhouse and stopped dead. "Cocksucking, motherfucking piece of shit" zipped through my head. *Falconry's* mast lay strapped to the deck. My hands shook with the effort to control my temper: the audacity. No matter, I thought — it will take some time, but I'll just put it up again.

The boat sat on her cradle. I pulled out the ladder from underneath her and climbed aboard. Standing on the deck, I took in the sweet air and sun, feeling some of the tempest drain away.

Preparing to hoist the thirty-foot mast again, for it was no small job, I unstrapped it from where it had been secured. Next I began checking to ensure all the rigging was present and untangled.

"Motherfucker," I hissed under my breath.

The rigging, six wire cables that held the mast in place, was gone. This was intolerable. There is a code among sailors. Number one, you do whatever you can to help a sailor in distress, so long as it does not endanger yourself or your crew. Number two, you do not, under any circumstances, touch another boat without permission.

It was all too clear. My uncle had known I would attempt to sail out of here. The mere thought that he had wrapped my prized possession under his control while I had been unable to do anything about it finally pushed my temper over the line.

I looked over my beautiful craft, her mast lying haplessly on the deck. I felt as though my wings had been clipped, and with this a wave of exhaustion rolled over me. The days of no sleep, little food, and hypervigilance had taken their toll. I slipped through the hatch into the cabin. It was a Spartan arrangement, a stripped-bare cabin with no amenities and only a couple of benches. One had to move bent double or on one's knees while inside.

I crawled up into the forepeak, curled up on the one cushion in the bow, shoved a sail under my head, and went to sleep.

* * *

I awoke with a sheen of sweat over my body. The air had become stuffy, heated by the freshly risen sun. The cabin had a light glow as the sun streamed gently through the hull. I unbuttoned the hatch and shoved my head into the open air, breathed deeply, and felt the sun strike my skin. Then I stood up straight, exposing my upper body above the deck. The light wind felt cool, drying my skin, but like the line of a squall, rage struck me, darkening the beautiful day.

I decided to go for walk. I needed to dissipate my emotions. My body was riveted with energy. I struck out for downtown. Only the more I walked about the city, the more I noted that the energy did not diminish. I meandered here and there, and over the hours my feet began to hurt, then to blister. Yet still I walked.

Occasionally I would see a one-way street sign and turn to follow the arrow. It seemed easier than attempting to go in another direction than the sign suggested. Once I saw a sign on an antique store that read, "Please come in," and I felt compelled to do just that. I pressed open the splintered wooden door and a small bell fastened above tinkled an announcement of my entry. That is, in retrospect, it must have been a tinkle, but to me it sounded more like a war drum, booming out the warning of enemy scouts on the ridge. Inside, cool, musky air assailed me. As I looked around the place, old, stacked pieces of furniture leaned against each other like old men hobbling down the street grasping each other for support. Atop every available surface was some kind of knick-knack, hundreds of little figurines or postmodern industrial ashtrays. There were little gnomes, ballerinas, farm animals, and fairies. It seemed this was the world depository for knick-knacks, the place where gnomes went to die. Each one with its bright colours, its odd costume, its actioned pose, clawed for the fullness of my attention. I could not disengage my mind. If I was able to wrench one off, another took its place. A cold sweat rose onto my brow, and my breathing became shallow. I thought I heard a little laugh and snapped my head around only to see a red-hatted gnome, a troll, and a pig dressed in a tuxedo gathered around a young farm woman pulling a bucket from a well. I could feel my face become hot, and I stepped back and thumped against a dresser, which was likely called an antique but only with a generous helping of imagination. I fled the shop with a panicky feeling lodged in my throat.

Toward sunset, my body still pumping energy, my brain fatigued — part of it yelling for rest, the other driving me to walk on — I paused to take in the thinning throng of people who remained on the street. I was standing on one of the city's main shopping drags. People's shadows were growing long and their faces were beginning to be obscured in the fading light. The witching hour, I thought. Suddenly I felt as though I were in a fantasy novel. My palms, and then my whole body, began to sweat — a cold, clammy sweat. I could not make out faces; people seemed to be sliding rather than walking along the street. I closed my eyes and rubbed my temple in an attempt to arrest this impression.

When I opened my eyes, I saw a tall, lean man in a dark suit and burgundy tie walking down the block toward me. He wore a black trench coat over his suit. I was captivated by the sight of him.

"Evil!" screamed my brain at me.

Ridiculous, I thought.

"Then why is he wearing a trench coat in the middle of summer?" my brain shot back.

I squinted at the man in order to get a better view of him. As I did so, my chest began to lock up. I looked quickly about for the best direction of exit and made a hard right into a park. I rubbed my temples again as I pressed into the park, the sweet scent of fresh-clipped grass momentarily elixed my nerves.

I glanced at a young couple sitting on a picnic bench nearby. Nothing suspicious there.

I glanced to the other corner of the park and saw two overweight men wearing Greek fisherman's hats. Their shadows extended deep into the park, longer than seemed correct to my eye. What could they be hiding? Demons, perhaps? I laughed at the thought, my gaze sliding off the men. When I reacquired the men in my vision, both stared blankly back at me, pale flesh clinging to their faces, pooling beneath their eyes into waddling jowls, their eyes chasms of darkness.

What in the name of all that is holy?! How could they hear my laugh from that distance? I made a hard turn back out of the park.

As I stepped onto the street, the otherworldly atmosphere vanished, instantly replaced by a much more ordered and civilized feeling. Odd, I thought. I took one step back onto the grass of the park.

In a rush, the feeling again morphed. I felt the breeze against my cheek, became aware of the sun low in the sky; my sense of smell seemed to become more accurate, and I thought I could detect the light purple scents of the flowers in the nearby garden.

I stepped back onto the sidewalk, and *bang*, those impressions were again replaced with civilized feelings. I stood there feeling both immense curiosity and something approaching sheer panic. These two emotions seemed to balance me out or, alternatively, paralyze me. It was hard to tell. Regardless, I stood rooted to the sidewalk unable to move or compute my experience. The darkening sun turned a deeper colour as it lowered in the sky and lit me in an orange haze.

Out of the corner of my eye I noticed one of the men across the park again turn to stare at me. What the fuck are you looking at? I thought. That's the way you want to play it? The anger welled up within me with surprising force and spurred me into action. I squared up on the man and locked my gaze with his. Nothing happened for a long moment, then I tilted my head minutely askew ... and the man suddenly found his shoes to be of great interest. After a close examination — to ensure they were still on his feet, I figured — he turned back to his companion.

I walked a few steps on, but was left unsettled. After staring at that translucent warbling flesh, I could not help feeling somehow that my actions had been unwise. I turned my back on the park. A black cab slid up to the curb in front of me.

"Taxi?" said the driver through the open passenger window.

With a vortex of emotion swirling within me, and with my blistered feet, I felt it best to vacate the premises. I climbed into the back of the cab and gave the address of the yacht club, and we were off.

I exhaled my body into the thick leather seats, becoming aware that the driver was chatting aimlessly at me. I did my best to ignore him and focused on the city outside the window, both to distract me and in the hopes that the driver would get the message that I did not wish to speak. Night had fallen over the city, and the lighted windows of the buildings and the passing car lamps gave the view a peaceful air.

The car made a right turn to head down to the waterfront and came up short behind a line of traffic. The pleasant view out the window was replaced with the sight of a massive Gothic church bathed in yellow light. I leaned over to take in the spire, which plunged up into the black sky. I stared at the long, thin, slit windows, the massive oak doors bound in iron, and the crosses littered about the structure. Just when you thought you had seen them all, the architects manage to stick another one in to surprise you.

I drew my gaze back to take in the rest of the church, and as I stared, the entire structure pulsed under my gaze.

"Whoa," I breathed, sliding back hard into the far corner of the cab, driving my body between the door and the black leather seat. The view of the church now safely hidden by the roof of the taxi.

I sat there for a moment, breathing — my arms pressing against the window and the seat back. Then, in tiny increments, as if having spied a firing squad waiting in ambush and driven by some perverse desire to see if they were still there, I slowly peaked under the taxi roof.

I blinked at the monstrous structure: inviting it, challenging it to shudder again. The more I stared, the more my gaze was drawn to the crosses, the stained glass, the high windows, and I became aware of the mythology of Christianity raging through my mind — the mythology no Westerner can escape — and I was surprised how much I knew. The knowledge emerged from my mind in the form of quotations, scripture, and images of ritual.

The taxi gently started forward, and as we drew away from the church, I twisted in my seat to watch the stone structure recede. Strangely, as it fell away, I could not help but feel that some answer lay there for me, an answer to all that I had been experiencing of late.

I straightened out and lay back in my seat. I caught the driver staring at me in the rear-view mirror. When our eyes met, the driver refocused on the road.

I noticed a wooden cross hanging from the mirror on a beaded tether. I glanced back at the driver. He seemed to be emanating a slight white light. If pressed, I might even call it an aura. No way, not possible, I thought. The idea of what I was seeing troubled me. I knew it was coming, and I tried to force it down, not allow it to enter my mind, but it pressed through anyway: an angel.

I closed my eyes and tried to process. I felt the need for reprieve, for the feeling of a warm body beside me. But that was closed to me now. I had closed it. As I thought this, I became aware that the driver was speaking to me.

"Pardon?" I said.

"Jazz. You like jazz?" said the aura-imbued driver.

The ineptness of the question, when held against all that I was thinking about, was rattling.

"Jazz? Sure, I like jazz. As much as the next guy anyway."

"I love jazz. I just start listen to jazz. In my country we don't have a lot of jazz. Maybe not enough people like it, so too expensive to put on radio. You know, people have to listen to put on radio."

As the driver spoke, I stiffened and began patting my pockets. I did not have any money to pay.

"Anyway," continued the driver, drumming the wheel, "I love jazz — such great music."

"Listen," I said. "I have a bit of a problem."

"Hey, man! Don't worry. If you have a problem, my friend, He will take care of it. Take care of all you problems," said the driver, gesturing with his head to the cross swinging from the mirror.

An interesting idea sprang to my mind, one that pulled at my thoughts and one I could not deny, an experiment, and I considered: If this aura-imbued driver really was an angel (the thought annoyed me but still wrangled me) and had intentionally picked me up to take me away from the park, and he had intentionally driven me past the church, then this was some sort of plan. If it was a plan, whoever made the plan must know that I have no money, and by extension this driver must know I have no money — which is what he meant by "Don't worry." Thus the driver was speaking in some sort of code, and this all ultimately meant that I need not worry about paying him. As far-fetched as this might seem, it had a kind of symmetry that appealed to me, and the only way to be sure was to test out the theory.

I watched the driver manipulate the vehicle through traffic, and listened to him drone about jazz. His movements were smooth and practised, but there seemed to be a delay between his inputs and the movement of the car, giving an eerie quality to the vehicle-driver relationship.

I continued to watch, wide-eyed, though slightly more relaxed now that I had resolved to test my plan.

When we reached the gate of the yacht club, I looked around. There was not another car or person around. One side of the cab was flanked by black water. The slight waves caught the moonlight, giving the impression of whitecaps in the gentle breeze.

"Here you are," said the driver.

"Thanks," I said. I slid across the seat; opened the door; climbed out; slammed the door; covered the space to the gate in two steps; punched the code; walked five or six steps; made a hard right behind a utility shed that was shouldered with thick green foliage mixed with overgrown vine roses; and waited, pressing my back against the rough planks of the door. I heard the heavy gate slam closed, the chain-link rattling in protest at its mistreatment.

There I stood for a few long moments. My back to the shed, hidden from view, the breeze gently rustling the leaves behind me. Nothing else moved. Quietly, I got down to my knees and poked my head around the other side of the shed. Through the large, waxy leaves, I could just observe the front gate. The black taxi stood there quivering as its engine rumbled inaudibly. After a moment, the light atop the taxi flipped on and the car drove smoothly away.

An angel indeed, I thought, my face pressed into the leaves. I suppose He will take care of everything?

The soft breeze intensified and shifted direction; it licked at my face and carried on it the scent of roses and the stink of the lake.

[CHAPTER SIX]

Once more unto the breach, dear friends, once more.

— William Shakespeare, *Henry V*

Through the darkness I headed to my boat, the gravel of the lot jarring my feet, thinking all the while, I need a drink. Passing the clubhouse, which loomed beside the glassy water, I made a sudden change of direction. I crouched low and ran to the steel staircase leading to the restaurant patio, and in a sweeping movement, I silently ascended the staircase.

The light of the city reflected off the grey concrete, bathing the atmosphere in a pale blue hue. I felt as if I'd stepped into a 1920s sci-fi movie. The closed restaurant waited in stasis behind dark windows. Having been a member of this club since my youth, I had learned a few things about the place. I slipped quietly along the patio to the restaurant entrance and gently pulled the door. The lock caught against its housing. I stood and braced myself against the ground, grasped the door handle, and looked quickly around. Assured of my solitude, I yanked. The lock slammed against its housing and popped open. The resulting crack echoed around the harbour like a pistol shot.

I stood looking over the boats in the harbour, attempting to sense any movement.

Satisfied that the sound had not drawn any attention, I tiptoed into the restaurant. What light there was inside filtered in through the high windows, partly outlining the tables, chairs, and bar.

Crouched low so that my silhouette would not be seen from the harbour, I padded across the carpeted floor to behind the bar. I was struck, as usual, by how the back of the bar bore no resemblance to the front. It was a kind of illusion, the bar, one that hid the relationship between drug and pusher. It was an illusion shattered when I glimpsed the business side of a bar. The resulting truth was one I found offensive.

I drew my attention over the mirrored brass shelves of booze displayed against the window. I selected a half-full bottle of half-decent rum and liberated it from its incarceration.

Moving low, I returned to the patio. I slowly closed the door behind me, the lock closing with a barely audible click. That click sounded as loud to me as a gunshot crack. I stood unmoving by the door for half a minute, then casually walked down the staircase to my boat.

I pulled the ladder from the trailer, leaned it against the hull, and clambered aboard, rum in hand.

In the cockpit, the hard aggressive bench doing little to alleviate my fatigue, I took a long swig from the bottle, drinking in the hopes that the alcohol would deaden the thoughts that continually threaded and knit themselves into my consciousness: the church, the taxi, the driver ...

Knowing, of course, that booze is a fool's games, I took another long bite of liquid anyway and looked straight up into the black sky, the liquid painfully burning its way down my throat.

I secured the cap and let the bottle fall from my hand. It banged and rattled its way around the cockpit, then came to rest in the stern, the brown liquid still sloshing around inside the bottle unaware of the stop in motion. I stared at it. I could not help but make a comparison between the roiling brown liquid and my own thoughts.

Descending into the lightless interior of the boat, I closed the hatch behind me. The boat formed a secure cocoon around me, and I lay down on the nearest bench for what was sure to be a fitful sleep at best.

* * *

Soon after the sun had risen over the horizon, the light of its rays warmed the interior of the boat and permeated the fibreglass hull, bathing the interior in a pale glow.

I awoke with a sheen of sweat covering my body. I had slept poorly, and I rubbed my neck in an attempt to dissipate the knots that had gathered there.

The night had been rife with disturbing dreams, and when one woke me, my mind soon went to thinking over the events of the day before until again exhaustion took me. Near morning I had resolved to investigate the impression I had had at the church. Now I looked down at my feet as I lay on the hard bunk. They were red and swollen. Worse, my heels both had large blisters.

That could be a problem, I thought.

I rummaged around in a locker beside my berth and withdrew a sailing knife and electrical tape. In a few moments I had lanced each blister and formed a rudimentary field dressing over my heels using electrical tape. I pulled on my socks and shoes, then pressed my feet against the floor to test the dressings.

Will have to do, I thought, and with that, I hoisted myself out of the boat. I headed out of the club and in the direction of the church, my feet whining their protests. The sun rose a degree and lit the water in a deep navy blue. A strong wind whipped up the surface of the lake and unsteadied me as I went.

* * *

Striding out in the direction of the church, I began to feel the twinge of desire for a cigarette. I patted my pockets in the vain hope of discovering a packet there, and the memories of the taxi from the evening before again flooded into my mind. I considered the taxi driver's words: *He will take care of all problems.* This idea seemed to have a strong pull on my mind; I could not seem to rid myself of it. I was walking through a small parkette now, and I tried to enjoy the trees, the grass, but my thoughts continued to return to those words.

Damn, I could use a cigarette, I thought, and I stopped short. Lying in the grass at my feet, held up by six long grass blades, like a talisman revealed after a long and arduous quest, was a cigarette, albeit partially smoked.

I picked up the cigarette and brushed some dirt from the tube. I dug in my pocket a came up with a lighter, lit the cigarette, and inhaled deeply. As I blew out smoke, I remembered a book I had read long ago, called *The Alchemist*. As I recalled, the book dealt with signs: if you followed the signs in life, you would be led to your true life's purpose, and if you did not, well, then, of course, all kinds of misfortune and unpleasantness would ensue. The novel had been immensely popular, one of those novels that even people with no interest in books read. The only problem with the novel, and the reason I had felt it rather trite, was that it required a religious temperament as a precursor — a temperament I most certainly did not have.

But as I stood there in the park, smoking a cigarette that had appeared at the mere thought of one, I began to wonder. A trickle of thought began to panic at that wonder, observing my other thought as though it were a small child wandering toward a roaring fire. But the majority of my mind would not let go. What if ...? What if? The theory could not be proven in either direction, so why not try to follow the signs, see what there was to see, and why not today? As Thomas Jefferson said, "Never put off to tomorrow what you can do today."

With that thought, I again struck out in the direction of the church, following the signs.

The walk to the church that was supposed to take no more the twenty minutes ended up taking over three hours. The moment I began following the signs, both literally and figuratively, I felt compelled to follow them. I would come to a one-way sign, a stop sign, a no-left-turn sign, a no-standing sign, and I was driven to follow them.

I attempted once or twice not to follow their directions, but this produced such tension within, such turmoil, that it was simply easier to move as directed. It was as though once I had made the decision to follow the signs, I was unable to go back on the decision, unable to let it go.

The same was true of more figurative things: a breath of wind, a shadowed street, a car horn. These things all held some significance in my mind, and I interpreted them as a direction for a change in course or a change in speed. Once the thought had entered my mind, I felt powerless.

Reaching the yellow limestone church, my head buzzed with mental exhaustion and unrest, and my feet screamed in pain. The makeshift bandages had long since deserted my shredded heels. I plunked down on the steps in front. The church loomed high above my head, and I gazed up at its twin spires, dusted with green corrosion. Something about the place beckoned, and once again hoisting myself to my feet, I pushed the iron-bound oak doors open.

One door swung partially open easily, and I was confronted with a thick incense-laden atmosphere. In contrast to the bright morning outside, the interior appeared sickly black, or was it the incense that made my stomach turn? Gradually my eyes adjusted, and I stepped inside, allowing the door to close behind me. The piston system hissed above the my head, the modern technology jarring in contrast to the old door.

"Hello," I called out into the echoing chamber.

I walked down the plush red carpet between the pews.

"Hello," I said again, my quiet call echoing round the vaulted ceiling. Light filtered through the stained glass windows, bathing the chamber in yellow and blue.

The lack of any visible person and the unlocked front door gave the church an eerie quality. I half expected a zombie priest to come limping and moaning out of the confessional at any moment. Still, I padded down the aisle toward the stage or, as it is called in these circles, the altar. Behind the stage a raised wooden chair presided over the pews ranged before it.

Directly behind the chair rose a huge wooden cross. I felt somehow drawn to it. I walked slowly forward until I had to crane my neck to take the whole cross in. I stared up at it for a long time, seconds ticking into minutes.

Christ, I thought. What if all that is happening to me had led me to this point? What if there has been a purpose to it all? Some force has persuaded my uncle that I am ill, driven me from home — all so that I may come here?

The thought struck me hard as I stared up at that giant cross. Though the theory had plenty of holes, I would be the first to admit it had a certain symmetry that was pleasing, a symmetry that my mind devoured.

Out of the corner of my eye I saw the smallest of flashes. I turned my attention to a small door off the wing of the stage. Perhaps some rogue beam of light had caught the door handle?

I knocked gently as I opened the door, but there was no one in the room. Really more of a closet than a room: along one wall a rack, recessed into the wall, contained ornate costumes. Evidently, this was the priest's space for preparing for services. I ran my hands over the thick white robes and embroidered purple shawls. Though they looked ornate, they all felt cheap and plasticky under my touch.

Another wall was bare except for a mahogany stained cabinet. I tried its doors, but it was locked.

"A key, where can I find a key," I muttered. "I need a sign, something to tell me where this key could be." I looked about the small white room in vain. Finally my gaze settled on the robes hanging on the rack. They were organized in increasing order of formality, the first a plain white robe, the last a heavily pleated job draped in a deep purple shawl, embroidered in gold about its shoulders. Their neat organization seemed to almost form an arrow.

I smiled and ran my hand over the inside of the recessed wall, sliding the ornate robe out of the way. At about chest height, I touched a nail, hammered into the trim. I fingered a small key, pulled it off the nail, and dropped it into the palm of my hand.

"Imagine that," I said to the room at large, and slipped the key into the cabinet. With a satisfying click, it unlocked.

Inside stood a crystal carafe of red wine and a pile of white wafers on a silver tray. With a small pout, I took one of the wafers. It was round and plain. I've always wondered what these taste like, I thought. I took a bite of the wafer. It had virtually no flavour and was dry, so dry it seemed to strip the moisture from the lining of my mouth.

"Awful," I said, and looked around for a place to put the half-eaten wafer. Finding none, I delicately placed it back in the silver tray, albeit with the bite mark facing down.

At least there is some wine to wash it down with, I thought. Unlidding the carafe, I took in the bouquet of the wine and nearly gagged on the aroma. The wine had gone off long ago, but to be sure, and perhaps driven by some perverse distrust of my olfactory senses, I stuck my finger in the carafe and tasted the liquid off it.

This time I really did gag, and spat out the few drops of wine that entered my mouth right onto the grey industrial carpeting of the dressing-room floor. Not that there was much to spit out, for the wafer had well taken care of that.

For all this ornateness, they can't even have decent wine? I pity those who have to drink this in service. With a shrug I locked the cabinet, replaced the key, and left the dressing room. Back by the altar, I again stood next to the elevated chair. Why not? I thought, and ascended the stairs to settle into the hard, straight-backed chair.

I cast my gaze over the pews and felt the power of the position. It was truly a heady seat looking down over those rows and rows of uncomfortable-looking benches, and I felt more like a king than a priest.

I thought that God was the king and there can be no other kings, least of all a priest as a king. So why this elevated chair? Seems a bit much to preach "God, thy king" while sitting in the position of king. Nonetheless, I felt the power of the place, the power of that church with its beautiful three-storey stained glass windows, the organ covering the rear wall. I stood, descended the steps, and made my way down the aisle to the exit.

There, I stopped and looked back over the vaulted chamber. Perhaps I have got this Christianity thing all wrong, I thought — maybe there's something to it. Perhaps that is why I was led here ... I wonder what the procedure is for conversion to this faith? In fact, I'll have to take care of that the first chance I get. With those thoughts, I swung open the thick oak doors and breathed in the clear air of the summer day — glad to be free of the choking incense-laden atmosphere.

* * *

After I left the church, the incense sticking to my clothing and clinging to my nose hairs, I wandered aimlessly. Here and there I went, then down a side street to emerge at the intersection of a busy street. On the corner sat two aboriginal guys, their backs leaned up against the brick wall of a Beer Store as though they were required to be there to prop it up. They were both clearly deeply drunk and slurred out jokes to each other.

"Cowboy, got any money for food?" one called out as I passed. This seemed to be the funniest thing the other had ever heard in his entire life, and he grabbed his gut as he rollicked in laughter.

The one who asked the question just looked at me, with impressive stoicism. His eyes betrayed not a scrap of humour.

I replied in the only suitable way, despite its being completely untrue: "I'll have you know I am one thirty-second aboriginal."

This set them both off, and soon they each had an arm hooked around the other's shoulder for support as they laughed, until they were wiping tears from their eyes. I confess I didn't think it all that funny — funny, but not *that* funny.

"You should have a drink with us then!" said the one who had asked me a question. I began to think of him as Long-hair, because, well, he had straight, black, long hair.

"Do ... you ... have any money for beer?" he asked, trying in vain to suppress laughter.

I rolled my eyes and dug into my pockets, pulling out something like four bucks in change.

Long-hair hoisted himself off the ground, plucked the money from my hand, and tottered into the Beer Store. In a moment he returned with three cans of Molson XXX and tossed one over to me. I shrugged, sat down next to them, and busied myself with the task of propping up the wall.

The beer was perhaps the foulest concoction I had ever tasted, though I could tell immediately that it had an outrageously high alcohol content.

"To the white man who stole our land," said the second guy. His face was badly pock-marked, as though he had suffered at the hands of smallpox.

I raised my can to that one and took another swig of the beer. The heat of the day was beating down strongly now, and the cool can felt good in my hand.

"You see my face?" he said, gesturing at his face with his index finger. "These remind me of every time I have been fucked by the white man, his church, his police."

"His church?" I was having a hard time deciding if his reference was metaphorical or literal, but I thought I might have an inkling of what he was saying.

"Don't get him started on the church," muttered Long-hair into his beer.

"Yes, the church, the fucking church. They come to our lands, build their cathedrals, try to convert our children from our gods. Yes, those motherfuckers should be castrated. I tell you, every time they fuck with me, I get another one of these," he said and again jabbed his finger into his face.

"Take it easy, take it easy," said Long-hair. "Hey, Cowboy, got a cigarette?"

I hadn't had a cigarette since the morning, and in truth I wanted one rather badly now. The beer was calling to be accompanied by a smoke. I patted my pockets in pantomime of a vain search and shrugged my shoulders.

"Okay," he said. "Let me show you a secret. The white man is a gullible fuck, and since tobacco was our invention, we have a right to take it back. Go up to someone you see smoking and ask them for some change."

"I'm not doing that," I said.

"Wait, wait," he said, and took a moment to drain his beer can. Mine, by contrast, was only a third gone. "Go up to him and ask him for change, then he's going to say no. Then you say, 'You got a cigarette, then?' The guilt of not giving up the cash will compel him to give you a cigarette. You'll see — works every fuckin' time."

I eyed him suspiciously but stood up, dusted myself off, and scouted the passing foot traffic.

I spotted my quarry, a man wearing tight jeans and thick-rimmed glasses. I came up in his blind spot just as he was puffing a smoke to life.

"Got some change?" I said. He barely glanced at me and looked as though he was preparing to bolt.

"Um, no, sorry," he said.

"How about a cigarette?" I said, and it worked like a charm.

"Oh yeah, sure, no problem. Got it right here ..." He animatedly patted his pockets and produced a cigarette.

"You need a light?" he added. I pulled out my own and flashed it at him.

"Thanks, pal," I said, turning back to my drinking buddies. They were both doing that little Queen of England clap.

"There you go, my one thirty-second brother, you'll never be without tobacco again," Long-hair said.

I laughed at that. "Time for me to get on moving," I said. Part of me felt a little strange panhandling for money.

"Take it easy, Cowboy," he replied, and I meandered down the street, smoking my cigarette.

* * *

I walked through the city for the next few hours. Late into the night, I found myself walking along a trendy street littered with small clubs and restaurants. I paused outside the dark facade of a club. The windows were painted black and covered with chain-link. A rock riff layered in a repetitive dance line filtered out onto the street. A mass of about a half-dozen revellers, each tightly clad in leather, stood outside the bar smoking cigarettes.

I moved on, but a half block down, the strangeness of the place struck me again. I turned to look at it. A middle-aged man, brown skinned, his face weathered, stepped out of the bar. He carried a heavy wooden walking stick. I thought he moved a little too lightly, a little too quickly, to be carrying a walking stick, even though he stood with a small stoop in his back. He said a few words to the people outside the bar, turned, spread his feet wide apart, crouched very low, and swung the stick in front of him a few times. He allowed the momentum to carry the stick above his head, and then whipped the shaft down in, finishing with a thrust of the tip.

A phrase, "he feigned a cane," came into my mind. The man looked back at his slack-jawed, leather-enshrouded audience and laughed. Then he assumed his stooped posture and began to hobble toward me.

I leaned against the nearest wall, old brick that was beginning to become powdery with age. As the man hobbled past I said, "Nice cane."

The man looked up with humour upon his face.

"It's just a walking stick," he replied.

This close, I could see that the cane had a ball head that would hardly fit into the palm of a large hand. It looked like something that would be more at home on an aboriginal weapon of war. The shaft, a couple of inches thick at least, was overdesigned. Its upper half was covered with characters that evoked images of wizardry and magic.

"Uh hunh," I said.

The man continued down the street. I stirred myself from the wall and fell into step beside him. He shot me a inquisitive half-glance. I replied with the same humour-filled expression the man had worn earlier.

"Where did you get the stick?" I said.

"It's something I found and made myself."

"Ahh," I said. "You got a name?"

"Miguel."

"Philip."

Miguel wore dark clothing, a grey T-shirt under a black denim coat. His clothing was pushing down-at-the-heel but was by no means threadbare. His face was weathered and brown but not aged. The different elements of his appearance appeared to be in juxtaposition. For some reason I felt compelled to test him.

I shifted my weight backward, swung around his back, and fell into pace with him on his other side. Miguel never lost his affable expression. Should have known that move would not startle a person carrying a stick like that, I thought.

"Where are you from?" I said.

"Born in Peru. Come here when I was a kid with my family to escape some unpleasantness down there. Got a large family, seven brothers and a sister. Most live north of the city now," said Miguel. He spoke with a smoothness to his words betraying the remains of a South American accent.

"When I was young," he continued, "I was a bit of a hellraiser, until one day my brothers got together and kicked the crap outta me. I'm not upset at them — I had it coming — but to this day I walk with a bit of a stoop. That's why I carry this stick."

The man was beginning to babble — a bit more information than needed, I thought.

"That doesn't sound like a good solution to the problem, a permanent injury," I said.

"I had it coming, I had it coming."

"Hanging out in the dance club?" I asked. "What where you doing in there? A bit odd in there."

"I had some friends to meet."

A fifty-plus Peruvian man with a heavy walking stick in a room full of pale twenty-somethings — unlikely, I thought. I looked around the dark street. We were several blocks away from our original meeting point, and few people were on the street. I thought of Miguel swinging the cane outside the club. I took a couple of quick steps forward, swung around to face him, stepped again, turning, and ended up by his opposite side, completing the circle I had begun half a block earlier. Miguel watched me, unperturbed, with evident good humour.

"Why are you talking to me, anyway?" he asked.

"I like the look of your walking stick," I said.

"I'm not messing with you, haven't messed with your family. What do you want?"

I paused for a beat and said, "I told you, I like the look of your walking stick."

Miguel stopped, looked over the cane, and thrust it into my hands. It was as heavy as it looked. The ball of wood constituting the handle was a knot grown into the shaft, polished smooth. I had not been expecting the man to hand over the instrument of my curiosity. Holding it, it lost all interest for me. I wondered what had compelled me to talk to this stranger about his walking stick, however oversized.

"It's certainly a nice piece," I said, handing it back.

As I did so, I heard a police siren. I looked up. Two police cars, lights ablaze, slid into the empty spaces beside the curb in front of us. Two officers jumped out of the first car. The driver, the younger of the two, wore his black hair in a military cut. The second cop was taller and older, and he wore his grey hair uncaringly.

"You, sir, please move over there," said the younger cop, gesturing for me to stand against the wall.

Separate all parties at the scene of an incident, I thought. Policing 101.

"Certainly," I said, taking a few steps down the walk. I watched as the officers from the other car gestured for Miguel to move against the wall. He sat against it, just out of earshot.

The older officer stood next two me. The younger one faced me head on. He was a half head shorter than me. We stared at each other a few long moments. He look a bit like he was holding his breath, all puffed up. Finally, I decided to take control.

"I don't want to make a mistake here," I said. "I'm not sure what is going on, but I'm sure we can resolve it."

At my words, the officer visibly deflated. I noted with pleasure that the older one, who had appeared relaxed at the onset, still did. When I had been much younger, I had been discussing one of my uncle's criminal cases with him. I'd asked him what I should say if I ever found myself in a situation with the police. He replied, without hesitation, "Tell them you don't want to make a mistake." I'd had the opportunity to use the line a few times before now with intriguing results.

"We got reports that an old man was being beaten up on the street," said the young officer.

I suppressed a laugh, but not too much of it. "That's ridiculous. As you can see for yourself, there is nothing of the kind going on here."

The officer digested this. I decided to play a slightly overt card, but an effective one: "I'm just walking home to my yacht club, where I'm staying. We're only a few blocks from it now. I saw this gentleman and we started talking."

The officers looked back at me. The younger one appeared positively tongue-tied. I gestured to where Miguel sat a few metres away, half in the shadows against the wall, two officers standing above him. I was surprised to see how wretched he looked.

"Please wait here," replied the officer.

"Certainly," I said.

The young officer conferred with the cops speaking to Miguel. I stood and waited.

Shuffling back, the young officer said, "The old man says you were just talking. What are you doing out so late?"

I realized he was digging.

"Just taking an evening stroll, taking in the town."

"Fine, it's late, please go *straight* home. Goodnight."

"Goodnight," I said, vising my lips together so as not to add "moron."

I set an easy pace down the street. A block away, thoughts of Miguel quietly assailed me. It had been easy enough for me to disentangle from those police officers, but Miguel might not be in such good shape, and he was looking so awful sitting there on the ground with two officers towering over him. I suppressed a groan and walked back.

The two officers who'd spoken to Miguel were standing a couple of car lengths down, by their cruiser. They watched my approach. The other two were in conversation, crewcut with his back to me. The older one fell silent as I approached. I smiled and nodded at him.

"Excuse me," I said to the back of the young officer. "What happened to the old man?"

The young officer snapped around, wearing a look of incomprehension.

"What are you doing back here?"

I paused. The question seemed to be of little relevance — and a little idiotic, as I had just told him what I was doing. Late-night traffic trickled down the street, bathing us in an oscillating halogen glow as I considered my answer.

"Compassion," I said after a time.

Silence greeted my reply. Then the young officer visible bristled. He took two steps forward and pushed hard against my left shoulder. I stepped back with my left foot, half turning with the force of the thrust.

"Get out of here right now," I heard him say. "Go straight home. If we get any reports of someone in a yellow coat bothering anyone, causing any trouble, we're going to beat the crap out of them. Do you hear me?" I felt my blood boil. I whipped around and was treated to a view of the young officer's back as he retreated to his patrol car. I took in the older officer in my peripheral vision, then I squared up on the young officer.

"If you ever touch me again — ever — I'm going to end you. I'll have your badge," I hissed in a voiced designed to carry the space between us. I saw the words strike the officer's ears like short, deadly, black arrows, the top of his ears wiggling at the impacts. That was more surprising than being pushed had been.

Exhaling, I swung my gaze over to the senior officer, whose previous calm demeanour had been displaced by a look of disbelief. His look was affirmation enough for the indignation I felt coursing through my veins. I continued to turn, walking straight away from the officers and their cars. Crossing the street, I never once looked back.

I made for the water, avoiding the main thoroughfares, taking the most direct route through small deserted side streets, for I had begun to question the wisdom of yelling at people walking about with side arms.

As I passed through the tree-lined back streets, I recalled the countless times I had taken this route. The houses had always looked quaint and peaceful — tall hedges and manicured lawns. Now as I passed they looked dark and hostile, the occasional lit window contorting the structures into monstrous, hostile faces.

Coming to the water at last, I decided to forgo the boat. Enough, I thought. I found the boardwalk and then the gate to my uncle's townhouse. At his door, I pulled my keys out and considered a moment: I had not spoken to my uncle since our conversation on the hospital telephone, but the thought of another night on a hard bench in the humid belly of the boat was enough to compel me to enter.

I unlocked the door. It opened onto the heavily wooded living area with an open-concept kitchen. It was dark, but warm and inviting. Knowing my uncle would be sleeping, I stepped inside and called out, "Hello, are you here?"

After a few beats I heard some stirring in the back and Uncle came out wearing a blue bathrobe that barely contained his large belly.

"It's late," he said, predictably.

"I know, I just need to sleep," I said.

"Fine. We'll talk in the morning." Without further discussion, he turned and went back to his bedroom. I repaired to my room, closed the door, and lay on the bed fully dressed.

In the relative peace of home, I reflected on the evening. The incident with the police had been way over the top, and it still had my pulse beating quickly. I tried to think about the church, but the confrontation continued to overlay itself in my mind. My thoughts shifted to seeing my uncle with his large belly. Suddenly I was seized with a panic that he was not treating his body with respect — his unhealthy practices would surely lead to an early death. I paused for a moment. The irrationality of the thought was blatantly obvious. Still, as I lay there I could think of nothing else. I did not know if it was the residual adrenaline from the police confrontation, but my body became ridged with tension. The near panic would not subside; the intensity of emotion became debilitating. Finally, lying there, I called out into the darkness: "Uncle!"

"Uncle!"

I was fully aware that I was behaving like a two-year-old having a nightmare, but I could not stop myself.

"Uncle!" I sat on the edge of the bed. My uncle opened the door wearing the same dark blue bathrobe.

"What is it, Philip? What's wrong?"

I felt tears begin to roll down my checks.

"Your weight," I said. "You're vastly overweight. You're going to die."

"Calm down ... What?"

"You're not taking care of yourself?" Momentarily I was able to grasp the irrationality of this situation, but I was powerless to stop it. The intensity of emotion was driving me. My uncle sat on the edge of the bed.

"It's going to be fine, Philip. I'm just fine. It's very late and you're exhausted." He patted my back. "Try to get some sleep."

I inhaled deeply nodding through my tears at the wisdom of the words.

"Good. Now lie down and sleep," he said and waited as I dried my face. With a bare nod, he went out through the door, closing it after him.

I stretched out fully on the bed, which was, without question, more comfortable than a boat bench. I took a few more deep breaths, and without warning, clicked off into sleep.

[CHAPTER SEVEN]

Oh, a storm is threat'ning
My very life today
If I don't get some shelter
Oh yeah, I'm gonna fade away
      — The Rolling Stones, *Gimme Shelter*

I awoke with dark orange sun licking my face. Stumbling out of bed, I opened my door and walked down the hall past the bathroom to the kitchen. As I passed the bathroom, I glimpsed a woman's figure and backpedalled a step. It was my uncle's girlfriend, Delora, standing at the mirror, naked. I shuddered. There were some things you should never see, and I trotted fast for the kitchen, figuring the best things was to focus on making coffee.

Delora was a mousy woman, wearing her black and grey streaked hair in a boy cut, counter to any form of style. I'd had no idea she was at the townhouse. I had never much cared for her, and frankly, I had always thought my uncle could do better. A therapist by trade, her dinner conversation revolved around little else, and worse, she left little room for anyone else's opinions.

In the kitchen I started brewing espresso on the stove. The memories of the previous night still fresh, I hoped a bit of coffee would help set things right. As I put the espresso maker on the stove, Delora came out from the back in a loose-fitting T-shirt and shorts, walked through the living room and out the front door, and took up a seat on the front step without a word. Leaving the door open, she lit up a cigarette.

Odd, I thought.

Turning the burner to high, I enjoyed the aroma of the freshly ground beans and anticipated the pleasure they would bring. The scent of the coffee mixed with whiffs of the acrid cigarette smoke drifting through the open door.

I walked to the door and sat next to Delora, thinking a cigarette would be just the thing right now. She tensed as I sat down and turned away from me slightly. Puzzled, I tried a polite approach,

"Good morning, Delora."

Nothing.

I was about to speak again, but Delora turned on me.

"I don't want to speak to you right now," she said, and crushed out her cigarette, got up, and went into the townhouse. I was startled at her rudeness. A guest in what was still my home, she had tried to make me feel uncomfortable. Though I had to laugh at her uncouthness, it could not stand.

I sighed as I rose to my feet, like an arthritic warrior reluctantly called back to arms. I was going to have to set her straight, and I hadn't even had my coffee yet. In the living room, squarely in the centre, stood Delora in a loose impression of a karate stance.

"You're ill," she said, "very ill, and don't want to do anything about it. You're a coward, Philip." She looked vaguely humorous standing in the middle of the room, tiny and mouselike.

I was tempted to laugh, but I felt my eyes harden. This woman was supposed to be a doctor. What kind of doctor calls an ill person a coward? Furthermore, there was a time and place, not so long ago, you called a guy a coward and you got your head chopped off.

I paused for a moment, searching for the most devastating words I could find. Delora was a doctor and considered herself intelligent, but her intelligence was flighty and ungrounded.

"Just remember, Delora, I'm smarter than you," I responded and watched the words slice cleanly through her neck, from one shoulder to the next, like a gleaming blade. Her eyes rolled slightly backward in her head. When they came back and focused on me, acquiescence filled her eyes.

I turned on my toe and walked out the door, leaving it open.

* * *

Stomping down the boardwalk in the morning sun, sans coffee and cigarette, I reflected that I had been getting into a lot of confrontations lately. It was time to call in some bigger guns.

In a few blocks I came to a pay phone, dropped in some changed, and punched a number. The receptionist for my psychiatrist came on the line and I made an appointment for eleven, in a cancelled slot, saying it was important that I see Dr. Sheffield that day. The blue digital numbers on the phone read half past nine. I took in the light of the azure sky: it was a good day for a walk.

* * *

An hour later I sat in the waiting room of the psychiatry department of Our Lady of Mercy Hospital, on the west side of the city, waiting for Dr. Sheffield. I had been seeing her for a few years now. There was something about her style that allowed me to listen to what she said. This was no small feat because, I reflected, I hardly listened to anyone. For that reason, I had nicknamed her Dr. Sheriff. I had been waiting for only fifteen minutes but was finding it difficult to sit still. I fidgeted and twisted in my seat, seeking a comfortable position.

"Come on in, Philip," said Dr. Sheffield, appearing in the doorway.

Dr. Sheffield was a small person with cropped hair — not unattractive, but thankfully, as I often reflected, not my type. I rose and followed her down the hallway to her office. She wore an elaborately woven Tibetan shawl over her white blouse and black pants. Classy, I thought.

We sat in her small office. Dr. Sheffield sat in her desk chair in front of her L-shaped desk. I took one of the two chairs facing her. As usual, without preamble, we began.

"What brings you here today? Tina said it was urgent," she said.

"Not urgent. Important, yes, but not urgent." I fidgeted in my chair.

"Tell me about what's important."

I began to recount the events of the last few days. The police, the interaction with my father's girlfriend, the hospital. As I did so, I was aware that the words tumbled out at a high clip and I was unable to stop them or even slow them down. Dr. Sheffield listened without saying much, writing on her pad. When I finished, a silence hung between us.

She looked at me and I looked at her.

"Philip, I'll tell you what I see. You have high energy, can't sit still, and are having some difficult situations. I don't know if you are unwell but I will say this: I think it would be best for you to come in for observation."

With that she turned to her desk, opened a drawer, and pulled out a form with four carbon copies attached — all different colours: yellow, green, red, and blue. For the first time in twenty minutes, I was speechless. A protest formed in my mind and I opened my mouth to speak it, but Dr. Sheffield beat me to it:

"I know you are not interested in coming into the hospital," she said without looking up. "But it is the best place for you right now. You have no place to go, and here people can watch you to determine if you're ill. I think you should go to the new short-stay program. There are only nine beds in the unit, and you stay for only three days. Seventy-two hours."

She stopped writing and looked at me. "We've talked about this eventuality," she said, not unkindly.

"I need a few moments to think it over," I said. "Do you mind if I go for a cigarette?" I rose from my chair and towered over Dr. Sheffield for a moment, and she turned back to filling out her form in quintuplet.

"Take all the time you need," she said.

I turned out of the office and thumped down the four flights of stairs, taking the final flight two at a time. The sound of my feet striking the steel staircase gonged through the stairwell.

In the hospital lobby, I was about to step outside when I noticed an older gentleman down a hall locking the door of his office. I recognized him in an instant as my old meditation teacher. He was a lean man in his sixties, with thinning hair turned completely grey. He wore a blue dress shirt almost disdainfully. Over it, as though to compensate for the requirement of formal attire, he wore a checkered flannel vest. In his arms he carried a large empty water jug, the type one would take camping. In any other person's hands, the jug may have seemed out of place in those long, cold hospital corridors, but in his, it seemed apropos.

"Jack," I called, approaching him down the hall.

"Philip! How pleasant to see you. How are you?" he replied, shifting the jug to his other arm.

I paused to considered the question: to most people, it was perfunctory. No real answer was expected. To Jack, who taught mindfulness meditation, the basis of which was to be present

— present in the here and now, with whatever that may bring — the question held a level of sincerity that was unusual. I decided to make the most of the question and express my present dilemma. Along with that stream of thought, another feeling nagged at my consciousness: the perfection of meeting my teacher, someone whom I had considered a trusted adviser, in this difficult predicament.

"To tell you the truth," I said, "I'm not so good. I have a decision to make — a difficult one."

"Do you?"

I felt Jack's full attention focus on me. I felt the ability to communicate fully open before me. This was his skill, and it felt calming, like stepping into the eye of a storm.

"As you know," I began, "I first came to your program because of a diagnosis of bipolar disorder."

"I recall you were unconvinced of the validity of that diagnosis," he said. "How's that going?"

I found sudden interest in the tiled floor. It was always difficult for me communicate on this subject, but I didn't have the luxury to indulge these difficulties now.

"A good question," I said. "Some have said, shall we say, it has flared up. I can't speak to that, but I am certainly in a conflict with my uncle, with whom I live. I can't go home. In fact, I am living on my small sailboat. My doctor thinks I should check into the short-stay unit here at the hospital. I am ... uncertain ..."

"It appears that you are. Why are you uncertain?"

Jack had an aspect about him that was centred. At times he was infuriatingly centred. I felt that centredness now, and it would have been irritating if not for the fact that some aspect of it held room for opportunity. It was as though, in being centred, there was room *around* the dialogue, around the situation, to create a solution.

"I suppose," I said, "it's that it all has the tone of incarceration. I'm reluctant to give up my freedoms, and I'm concerned about what medicine they'll ask me to take."

Jack digested all of this. "Firstly, Philip," he finally said, "only you can decide what to take. It is what you have just said: 'ask me to take.' They may only provide suggestions, but as they are trained professionals, you may wish to gauge their suggestions as such. Besides, what is the problem with taking medicine? Look at me." I did. Frankly, he looked old, but lean and strong. He had taught mindfulness meditation to countless people and undoubtedly had helped many with severe issues. One would be wise to listen to his counsel, I thought.

"I take vitamins," he continued, "and that is because my body simply cannot make certain compounds for my body to function. How is your situation different?"

I felt a familiar flash of irritation. Certainly, vitamins were different from what they would ask me to take. Were they not? I inhaled sharply in a effort to control my temper, for I did not have they luxury of time to debate this issue.

"As for staying in the unit," Jack added, "you have said you have no place to go and everyone needs —"

Jack broke eye contact and cast his gaze about the hallway. He looked back at me smiling gently.

"— a container — a place in which to put themselves." As he said this, his gaze flicked down at the jug cradled in his arms. I looked down at the jug. Indeed, everyone needs some place to put themselves: their thoughts, problems, joys, belongings. When I met Jack's gaze again, I could not be sure, but I thought I caught a light in his eyes that had not been there before — a light that betrayed some deeper significance, deeper than mere chance at our meeting.

For a moment I said nothing, then I snorted a laugh.

* * *

I walked slowly back up the stairs to Dr. Sheffield's office, momentarily pausing at the doorway to observe her. The Sheriff sat diligently filling out the rainbow-coloured forms. I walked into the office and sat on the edge of one of the chairs.

"Time to get it done," I said. She looked over at me and nodded at the apparently forgone conclusion.

[CHAPTER EIGHT]

The ocean is so vast, my boat so small.

— Cape Breton fisherman's prayer

I watched as Dr. Sheffield finished filling out the unquestionably official forms.

"Ready to go?" she asked.

I nodded. Dr. Sheffield seldom acted so decisively. When she did, her actions spoke volumes. Yet even though she clearly thought I could use some form of assistance, I still observed a battle within myself, an unwillingness to admit that anything was wrong.

We stepped out into the hallway. It was surprisingly barren of people, and the utilitarian hallways did not inspire hospitality. I wondered why hospitals could never use warm paint colours or unabrasive lighting.

As we walked down the hallway, I became aware of the massivity of my frame next to Dr. Sheffield. I was close to a foot taller than her and, I reasoned, my perception was compounded by the fact that I almost always interacted with her while sitting.

"I just want to make one thing clear," I said while we rode the elevator up two floors. "I'm here as a voluntary patient, correct?"

"Correct," said Dr. Sheffield. "But Philip, I must encourage you not to leave until the end of the three-day period."

Exiting the elevator we took a left and came to a double set of steel doors. A sign hung above the door on thin metal chains:

Mental Health. Short-Stay Unit.

"Great," I muttered — always such charged nomenclature around here. It would be better if they used some kind of code. Like "Fuzzy, Comfortable Place to Rest Unit," but no.

Dr. Sheffield pulled a key card attached to a cord from her hip and passed it over the locking sensor. The lock clicked open.

We walked into the unit. I was taken aback by the cleanliness of the area. It was almost pleasantly utilitarian, in a vinyl-covered hygienic way. The room was hexagonal. In each of the eight corners were beds, some with their hospital curtains drawn, others empty. In the centre were a couple of couches, an armchair, and a coffee table covered with dogeared magazines. A long table, presumably for eating, dominated the room. One wall was made of glass, and behind it was an office where four people sat at desks. Adjunct to this area lay a small glassed-in conference room.

A robust black nurse came out from behind the glass wearing a large smile.

"This must be Philip," she said.

I was instantly suspicious. Her smile was disproportionate to the situation. I glance at Dr. Sheffield, who minutely shrugged her shoulders.

"I'm Terra, and I'll be your nurse for today," the woman continued.

"I'm Philip, and I'll be your patient for today," I said, sticking out my hand.

Terra froze with the smile plastered on her face. I looked back at the door. I saw no handles or breaker bars.

"I never agreed to be locked in here, Dr. Sheffield," I said.

"You are not locked in — you are a voluntary patient," replied Dr. Sheffield. "If you want to go out for a cigarette or take a short walk on the grounds, you are free to do so. Usually the policy of the unit is that you are required to sign out at the nurses' station, but that is a formality which does not pertain to you. Is that not so, Terra?"

"Of course," said Terra, having recovered. She now wore a more professional demeanour.

"I'll leave you to it," said Dr. Sheffield, handing Terra the rainbow forms. She shot me a quick smile and without further ado, swiped back through the doors.

I watched as the windowless metal doors swung quickly shut. I guessed that the rapidity of the closer was by design, so no one without authorization could slip through. With their clang, I realized I was again locked up, albeit to a lesser degree. I knew that the staff would be watching me through the glass and, should I make the wrong move, they would lock me up without hesitation.

I felt rebellion wash through me, obfuscating the reasons for my stay. I looked about the room and wondered why it was these places never had windows.

* * *

Terra got me settled in one of the empty beds, with sheets, a pillow, and towels. She also gave me hospital gown, saying that patients were encouraged to wear them. I shot her a look of incredulity that cut that dialogue short.

It was early afternoon by this point. After going out for a cigarette, and with nothing much to do, I sat on one of the communal couches and started reading a three-year-old *Economist* magazine. Oddly, I could not focus. After a few lines, I would get up, pace, sit, and try again. I thought of my papers lying on my desk in my uncle's townhouse. I thought of how I could not focus on my work, how my mind shot away at an attempt of focus. At these meanderings, a shudder of trepidation ran through my body. Again and again I tried to read, but my mind banged into strange and unrelated quarters. Frustrated, I tossed the magazine onto the table. It skidded over the tabletop, its pages fluttering.

I gathered a pencil and some scraps of paper from the table and sat to do some work. A top-40 radio station droned in the background. I attempted to block out the sound and tried to begin the composition of a poem. But every time I put my pen to the paper, the words I had held in my mind just seemed to skit away, replaced by the song on the stereo. My mind would latch onto the lyrics. What once I would have called the epitome of trite composition, noteworthy only for the heights of vacuousness achieved, now had an otherworldly ability to seize my thoughts. The words seemed to be profound, and I had to jot them down. A part of my mind knew that there was nothing earth-shattering in what I heard, and as I watched myself write furiously, lest it slip from my mind forever, I wondered what exactly the hell I was doing. Finally I had to tear myself away from the sounds, and as this sensible, aesthetic part of myself gained traction, I tossed the pen across the room in disgust.

Thinking that perhaps throwing sharp pointy objects around the ward was something the staff might look down on, I glanced up into the office, but it appeared that no one was paying me much attention at all. I looked straight up. Little black spheres were bolted intermittently throughout the ceiling. Curious, I took a turn past the nurses' station. Sure enough, two of the computer consoles were dedicated to video feeds from the unit's ceiling. I returned to my seat. Something about the covert observation angered me. I sat and pondered this emotion for a long time, massaging it, kneading it. Finally, unable to diminish its influence, I resolved that they would get nothing from me. Not a glimmer. I would sit, eat, watch some movies — and there would be nothing to see at all.

* * *

Late in the day, while I was pattering about the room, a man in a grey tweed coat and pressed beige slacks walk through the double steel doors. He did not look up but rather slinked into the nurses' station, his shoulders hunched as though he did not wish to be observed. His black curly hair was flecked with grey. A doctor, I thought.

The doctor sat in the glassed-in conference room and began flipping through a file. Presently, Terra informed me, "The doctor is in."

Dr. Sheffield had informed me that the unit was run by Dr. Katherine Wilcocks. I was unsure why I was going to have *this* meeting.

"I'm Dr. Charles. I'm the head of psychiatry here at the hospital," said the doctor, rising and extending his hand as I entered the conference room.

"Okay," I said, shaking the doctor's hand. I took the seat opposite.

"Dr. Wilcocks informed me that because you know her on a somewhat personal level, it would be a conflict for her to act as your doctor. She asked me to stand in her place," said Dr. Charles.

I recalled in a flash a meeting a few years earlier. Dr. Sheffield had asked me to meet with Dr. Wilcocks in regard to some medication issues. Upon meeting her, I recognized her from the yacht club opposite mine, a cruising club. I had often seen her relaxing on her boat in a bikini on the weekends — an orange bikini, if I recalled correctly. As the interview with Dr. Wilcocks had progressed, I had become unimpressed with her tone and let slip I had seen her on her boat from time to time. She became unsettled for a moment, staring off into the distance and muttering, "Oh, you can see me." After that the interview had progressed on a different track, and one more amenable to my taste.

"Of course, that's fine," I said, chuckling at the recollection.

"I've reviewed your file," said Dr. Charles. "Is there anything you would like to add that you did not discuss with Dr. Sheffield?"

I eyed the file lying on the table.

"No," I said. "I have told her just about all of it."

"Very well," he said, aligning the file with the edge of the table. "Dr. Sheffield thinks that you may be suffering from the early stages of mania, the high side of a bipolar condition, called hypomania. This is, as I am sure you know, characterized by heightened agitation, severe restlessness, and little sleep. Sometimes it can manifest in overspending, and people in this state often begin to abuse drugs and alcohol."

I nodded.

"If this is the case," he continued, "it is important to treat it early so that the condition does not progress to full-blown mania. I'm going to start you on a dose of valproic acid, a drug that should help stabilize your condition. Clear?"

"Why don't you tell me what you really think?" I said, and quiet descended over the conference room. I rolled up a corner of my mouth to help him along.

"Well," he began, "what do you want me to say, Philip? You know the score."

"Do I?" I said. "Okay. I'll ask you one question then, one no one has been able to answer for me. I am familiar with the drug you are attempting to prescribe for me. In fact, quite a few people over the years have attempted to prescribe it for me, but no one has been able to answer one simple question about it. I studied science in university, including biochemistry and microbiology. I've worked for some of the largest hospitals in this city, and I worked for an experimental biotech drug company in San Diego, so to me, this seems like a pretty important question."

"Yes?" said the doctor.

"How does it work?"

"Ah, let me explain it to you," said Dr. Charles, pushing back his chair. "Information gets stored initially in this hemisphere of the brain." He gestured to one side of his head, with a circular motion. "In an active hypomanic situation, the information does not get sorted out and stored in other parts of the brain. Instead, the information gets trapped, banging around in the original hemisphere. As more and more information gets input, the situation gets worse and worse. This is made worse by a inability to sleep because sleep is the time when major chunks of information are sorted and stored in the brain. This drug helps to facilitate the transfer of information to other parts of the brain."

I watched as the long-held question evaporated in my mind. It was like the tumblers of a lock falling into place.

"Simple as that ..." I said. "Why has no one told me this before?"

The doctor gave me a hapless look.

Trailing this logical and concise answer to a question that had eluded me for years lay a wake of clarity. In that clarity, I elected to follow the doctor's counsel.

"Fine," I said. "It seems like a good idea to do as you suggest."

"I'll give the nurse the prescription and we'll watch you for the next two days. After that, we'll see where you're at."

We left the conference room and shook hands. I watched the doctor walk out the doors of the unit and thought over our talk. Despite the conversation's positive nature, I felt annoyance flame. Who was this person to be prescribing medicine to me after such a short meeting? I was not ill — I had simply run into a lot of vexatious people lately.

I breathed deeply and was momentarily able to examine my annoyance: it did not make any sense.

* * *

The next morning I awoke and stumbled out of my hospital bed. The unit was awash with harsh fluorescent light. My breakfast was laid out on the communal dining table. No one was around except a couple of nurses in the station. I sat in front of my plastic dining set and lifted the plastic heat cover off my plate. There I discovered something that resembled scrambled eggs, the sight of which made my stomach turn.

At least there is coffee, I thought. Taking a sip of the insipid brew, I could tell immediately it was decaf.

"In the name of all that is holy," I muttered. Sleep still pulled at my mind. The strange environment in which I sat suddenly made me feel as though I was strapped to the inquisitor's rack. What am I doing here? I thought.

Images leapt into my mind of my sweet little sailboat laid up at the dock. I thought of sailing down the coast, coffee in hand. Surely that was better than being here? There was nothing wrong with me. This situation had simply spiralled out of control. I just needed to get away for a while. To do that I needed my rigging, and I knew where to get it.

I walked over to the nurses' station and informed them I was going for a smoke.

"So early?" said the attendant nurse.

"What can I say? I'm addicted."

The nurse pressed the electronic lock and I swung the heavy steel door open. I walked out into the hall, down three flights of stairs, through a side door, and onto the hospital grounds.

Taking in the warm summer day, I lit a cigarette and looked both ways down the street. I crossed the small space between the hospital and the street, and walked in the direction of the harbour and my uncle's place. I did not stop till I arrived.

I stood at my uncle's townhouse looking at the front door. Without my rigging I could not sail, and I knew who had it. I would get the rigging, come hell or high water. But first, a drink. I set out for the yacht club, leaving the door unaccosted.

And drink all day I did. I sat at the yacht club bar ordering glass after glass. At some point Stephanie arrived, and we drank. We drank as the sun went down and a band came and set up on the patio. I drank as we danced, the revellers in my peripheral vision a blur. Stephanie grabbed my hand and took me down to the dark harbour.

"Where are we going?" I asked.

"An owner lets me use his boat sometimes. If I'm working early, sometimes I sleep here. I know he keeps his boat unlocked."

I said nothing, letting the unasked question hang in the air.

"He wants to get into my pants," she said.

"Ahh," I said.

We stumbled down the dock to a beautiful forty-foot wooden yawl, painted white, her deck gleaming with polish. With a quick look, Stephanie jumped aboard and disappeared through the hatch. Without further thought, I followed her below.

The interior was as lovely as the exterior, all teak, navy blue cushions, and brass fixtures. I sat on the edge of a settee and tried to acquire Stephanie's eyes in the dimness.

"Look," I said, "I don't know. I think it's important to say I'm kinda with someone. I don't want to hurt them."

She turned then, ducking the light of my gaze. She opened a teak wall panel, revealing a tiny bar. I caught the twinkling of crystal. With the practised movements of a professional, she pulled out a glass, then an ancient-looking bottle of rum. She pulled out the cork and it made that wet popping sound that foretold pleasure. She glanced back at me then, perhaps just to see if I was watching, but there was no veiling the mischievous glint in her eye, nor the allure of her smile.

She poured a measure of the black-brown rum and replaced the cork with a squeak. Then she picked up the glass and stood there looking at me across the cabin, her hip jutted out, her fingernails tapping a gentle rhythm into the glass. I could not tell if she was appraising or admiring or simply trying to decide what to say.

She passed me the glass. The scent alone was enough to intoxicate.

"You are with someone or *with* someone?" she said, pulling down my pants and kneeling in front of me.

I was rather accustomed to more preamble before such action, but I discovered that with my pants around my ankles I had not much inclination for discussion. With the last vestige of strength I asked, "Do you have any protection?"

"What do we need that for?" she cooed, laying her check against my thigh. It felt ridiculously soft there against my thick muscle. As my mind began to lose all logical control, I wondered, is this what they meant by "unsafe sexual practices" ...?

* * *

I awoke feeling disgusted, but Stephanie's naked bosom pressed against my torso did help somewhat with that. I untangled myself from her embrace and soundlessly slipped out of the boat into the bright morning sun. Oddly, I could detect no evidence of a hangover, just a lingering fatigue. I needed to sail, to rid myself of those ill feelings. I needed to sail, and my boat needed her rigging — and I was ready to get it.

Within a half hour I was standing at the front door of my uncle's townhouse. I knocked, the door opened, and there stood he stood.

"Do you have any coffee?" I said. My uncle stared blankly back at me for a moment.

"You'd best come in," he said.

I sat in the heavily wood-panelled living room, where not forty-eight hours before I had had the altercation with Delora. My uncle poured me a cup of thick coffee from the stove. Handing it over, he sat on the couch opposite the chair I had taken. He wore pressed grey suit pants and, I noticed, a startlingly white shirt. Silver cuff links gleamed subtly in the fresh sun. Warrior's dress, I thought.

"I thought you were in the hospital," he said.

"How did you know that?" I said.

"The hospital had me on file as the next of kin. They called me last night."

"I'm done with that place," I said, taking a swig of the excellent coffee.

My uncle leaned over his coffee cup and said nothing.

"What I need is my boat," I said. "I need to get away for a while. This thing —" I gestured around the room, "— has spiralled out of control. I need space, and you have my rigging. I want it back."

My uncle sat still, and said nothing.

"What you've done is wrong," I continued. "You have stolen my property. That is *illegal*. And while I'm on the subject, I have to say, you are some piece of work. A suicide note — that was creative. I wonder, did they eat it up when you called them? 'Dear Sir!' did they say? 'We'll put everyone we have on it!'"

My uncle shrugged his shoulders, and I could not be sure, but I thought I saw a hint of a smile. "I did what I had to do," he said.

"Don't you get it?" I said. "The more you push, the worse it gets. I'll tell you this one time: You can only push so much before people start to push back."

"Philip, I really think you should consider —"

"I don't want to hear what you think is best," I said. "I have no desire to have this conversation with you. If you want to talk, give me my rigging — then we can have a discussion."

"I'm not going to do that."

I moved to edge of my chair. I felt as though anger began to singe the tips of my hair.

"It's mine," I said. "You have no right. How would you feel if I took a baseball bat to the windshield of your car? How would it feel, what would you do?"

"I would call the insurance company and get it fixed."

I let out something between a growl and a sigh.

"Give it back, Uncle."

"I won't do that, Philip. You might be quite ill, and who knows what could happen out there?" He gestured out past the harbour.

Rage sprang into me. I flashed to my feet, grabbed the coffee table, raised two legs into the air, and smashed the table back onto the ground. I knew I was breaking all familial protocol, but the potency of my rage was unmanageable. If I did not give it some expression, I would literally explode.

"Give me my property," I growled. "What do you know of illness? Who are you to say I'm ill?"

"Calm down, Philip," he said, having barely moved an inch, still holding his coffee cup in both hands. "Let's take a walk and talk it out."

Gripping the coffee table with white knuckles, I considered, and then sank back into my chair.

"Let's go talk about it then," I said. My uncle rose from the couch and retrieved his suit coat.

* * *

Outside, we began walking toward the park. Silence hung between us like a protective curtain. The park lay next to the water, tucked away from the seething metropolis and hard to reach. It consisted of a stand of large pine trees, each forty feet high. The atmosphere of the place vacillated between foreboding and peaceful. My uncle and I walked into the stand. A mat of pine needles covered the ground releasing their waxy scent.

"I know you think there may be something wrong with me, Uncle," I said, "but I"m fine. I've said before, I just need some space."

"Philip," Uncle said on a exhalation. "You are not well ..."

At these words I felt my temper rise. The trees seemed to grow larger, to pulse. I rubbed my temples in an effort to eviscerate the image. This is enough, I thought. I have to do something to illustrate that this conversation is not one I wish to have.

"I am not interested in the commentary," I said. "Enough. Enough. Enough! I'm sorry." I moved a step closer to my uncle to give him a hug before I left. As I did, I saw in my peripheral vision my uncle's arm come down from high above his head. Later I would suppose that he meant to come and give me a hug, and I would happily believe that to be true. To me, though, it seemed too high, moving too fast. Was it moving to slap me? I circled my left arm around and over top of my uncle's outstretched arm as it came down, then grabbed his wrist and turned slightly. I knew my uncle had studied judo at one time. Now, he turned my wrist to break the hold. He was fast, but not fast enough. The hold was broken slightly, but it placed his arm in a more vulnerable position. I readjusted with my left hand and covered with my right while taking a step forward. This unbalanced him. I prepared to throw him to the ground ... one more step and he would be in the dirt.

"Philip, what are you doing? I'm your uncle!"

I paused, released my grip. I was bewildered by my actions. The pressure, stress, adrenaline welled up inside me.

"I'll be at the harbour," I said. "You'll know where to find me." Without looking at my uncle, I stalked off, the sky above my head roiling with billowing thunderheads.

* * *

I punched the code at the harbour entrance and smashed through the gate. I reached my boat, my last place of refuge. I climbed on board her beautiful white hull, unstrapped her thirty-six-foot length of mast from the deck, and lashed a line to it. Then I unceremoniously lowered the mast to the concrete below.

Climbing down, I grabbed a trolley, attached it to the front of the trailer, and pushed the two tons of boat down the slight grade to the launching crane. Connecting the heavy steel hook to the lifting strap inside the boat, I punched the lift button. The industrial electric winch creaked as it took up the weight.

I swung the boat over the water and lowered her in. She welcomed the water, elegantly displacing the lake around her waterline. I did not know what I was going to do next. I would paddle her if I had to — I just had to disappear. Mortification at my actions drove me on. I disconnected the steel hook and swung the crane out. I climbed back onto the sleek deck and crouched over the mast hole to examine it for obstruction.

"Philip," a voice said to my back.

The fallout.

I turned and was confronted with a view of four female police officers standing in a fan formation. Off to the side stood a chunky blonde wearing a bulletproof vest that read "NURSE" across the front. Her vest contorted her weight and spilled it out in unnatural ways. It was the same obese woman I had seen in front of the hospital.

"Yes," I said.

"Your uncle has called us," the nurse said, "and said that you're ill and you need to see a doctor. You must come with us."

"That is untrue," I said while taking in the situation, calculating. "My uncle attempted to strike me. I defended myself. He has simply activated you for his design. It is a lovely day, and I am working on my boat. I am not going anywhere with you."

"You may be just working on your boat, but we must take you to be examined."

I wondered what qualified this overweight woman to pass comment on whether or not I needed to be examined when she could so evidently not take care of herself. I considered a comment to that effect, but it would be so grossly unkind. I let the obvious hang in the air a moment while I gazed at her frame.

"You and I both know that you are bound by the rule of law," I said. "Stay off my boat. Leave. I am not going with you." I glanced again over the evenly spaced women who had still said nothing.

My eyes came to rest on the woman in the centre. From the front of her uniform belt protruded the yellow and black barrel of my old acquaintance, the taser. The mere sight of it made me bristle.

"Can't do that," the nurse said. "We're not leaving till you come with us. You have to be checked out by a doctor, and then you can come back and enjoy the rest of the day. Please, get off the boat."

I had heard that line before.

"I'd sure like to hang out by a boat today," said one of the cops said, casting her eyes over the blue sky, not paying much heed to the storm clouds forming in the distance.

"Nice day," replied another.

I considered my options for evasion. I could charge through their rank. I might make it through, if I didn't get tasered, or, for that matter, shot, but I would not get far, for I was sure the squad cars were close by, and there was a large stretch of road between the harbour and the city.

I looked at the blue, sun-flecked water of the harbour. I could dive off the boat. Unfortunately, the only place I could swim to would be the docks, which all led back to a spot not twenty metres from where I stood now.

"Philip," the nurse said, "we are not leaving till you come with us. We'll wait all day."

"Wait as you like." I turned my back on the troop, walked to the bow, and sat cross-legged facing the lake. I will not allow these people to make a decision for me, I thought. I closed my eyes and breathed deeply, feeling the anger, adrenaline, and injustice rich in my veins.

I breathed again — I thought of my boat and the water beyond.

I breathed again — I thought of the police behind me, and my anger pulsed, squeezed through my capillaries. I raised my arms in an L shape beside my body, flexed my back, shoulders, and arms, and felt the muscles pop beneath my T-shirt.

Bringing my arms down into my lap, I laid my palms upward, one in the other, and I breathed again ... and again.

"Philip, you must get off the boat."

I breathed.

"What is he doing?" said one of the officers.

I breathed.

"He's meditating," said the nurse. "I'm going to have a seat."

I breathed.

This situation was out of control. It is unlike me to be anywhere near such a situation, to allow such things to happen. The only choices were to swim across the harbour or go with them.

I breathed.

Go with them, I thought. I felt the air flow though my nostrils.

I opened my eyes and adjusted to my surroundings. I took in the lake, the sun, and the water. I felt calm, ready. Slowly, I rose to my feet and turned. One of the officers stood half off the dock, her leg swinging over the rail of the boat. As her boot touched the deck, I cringed. It was like a bass drum being struck in an empty concert hall. The boot was a big official affair with soft black rubber soles. The scuff marks on the gleaming deck would be awful.

The gall, the insult. I briefly considered taking two large steps and flicking the woman into the water. She would not stand a chance. This was my boat, and I knew her well — and with all that gear strapped to the woman's waist, she was helpless. As these thoughts streamed through my mind, I glimpsed in my peripheral vision a police boat rolling through the harbour entrance. If they wanted a show of force, they would get a show of force.

"*Hai!*" I bellowed in guttural Japanese, swinging my leg back, squaring up on the officer in the middle of the fan formation and raising my arms in a defensive position.

No one moved for a moment — then three hands went to the butts of their side arms. The officer in the middle ripped the taser from her belt and trained it on my midsection. I looked her in the eye and saw fear licking at her mind.

I no longer could see the black and yellow of the barrel. I saw the rectangular bore trained on me. The bore, covered by four equal-sized triangular pieces of plastic, was recessed slightly into the barrel, which, I supposed, sprang back when the projectile was fired.

Enough.

I dropped my arms to my sides.

"Right," I said. "Let's go."

[CHAPTER NINE]

There must be some way out of here, said the joker to the thief
There's too much confusion, I can't get no relief
— Bob Dylan, *All Along the Watchtower*

I was chatty and boisterous in the back of the police car. It became clear by their route that they were headed back to the same hospital they'd taken me to before.

They processed me at the hospital triage station, which took longer than I expected, being surrounded by two police officers and an obese nurse in a bulletproof vest.

The officers left me in the same dingy unit with the same heavy locking door. I sat again in an overstuffed vinyl throne staring at the glassed-in nurses' station.

I sat rigidly straight in the chair, staring down anyone who looked in my direction. After a time no one looked at me at all. Probably not a good way to engender equanimity, I reflected, but I no longer cared. Thunderous emotion clouded my thought.

Inside the station were four nurses dressed in white or blue scrubs, a couple of support staff in green scrubs bringing in the afternoon meal, and two security staff dressed in black polos. They reminded me of overweight zoo gorillas, for both looked ready to begin drooling at any second. They have brains to match, I thought. One of the guards had grey streaks on either side of his curly hair, making him look slightly more distinguished than the other, who was bald.

I sat in my chair for a good twenty minutes, with nothing much happening at all. In the midst of my observations I watched as another patient, a small and slender woman with straight black hair and a neat red skirt, walked up to the window of the nurses' station. She began a conversation with a nurse. As I watched, the conversation became more animated, though it was conducted in low tones. I wondered what could have occurred to bring her to this place.

With no apparent cause, the woman turned and bolted at full tilt. The nurses' station door slammed open and the security guards rushed out. I could not believe what I was seeing: a pair of two-hundred-pound men chasing a woman who looked to be no more a hundred pounds, and that on a good day. I dreaded the scene that would occur if they caught her, and it was inevitable, for the room was about as big as a closet.

In my book, one did not violently chase down a woman, and I reacted fast. Before the guards had lumbered two steps, I had planted myself directly in their path.

They stopped dead less than a pace away from me, one standing behind the other. I was aware it was not a strong tactical position — they were too close — but what could I do?

I looked from one guard to the other. The guards looked back with indecision. For a long moment there we stood — I barely saw it coming: the punch. It came over the shoulder of the guard standing in front of me, thrown by the guard behind, his fist obscured by the other's black uniform. My lip smarted. A lame punch, really, I thought I brought my hand to my lip and felt a small trickle of blood. I licked the blood from my finger. The salty taste struck my palate, and I turned my gaze fully to the guard who had thrown the punch. I gazed with the full force of the incredulousness that flowed through me. He looked back blankly, like it was taking him a long time to process what had happened. The other guard looked at me in surprise, his paws swinging down to his sides.

There we stood for a few long moments. Then, as if cued by a director offstage, both started grappling at my clothing. Unbelievable, I thought. The scene had a sense of the unreal, for though they grabbed at my clothes, they did not move me, nor did I move. It was as though their hands were repelled by a magnetic force.

In a way, I felt my task to have been accomplished: their focus was distracted from the woman. A layer of my mind noted this and released.

By the guards' movements, it was apparent that they wanted to move toward a door with a small, square, glass window reinforced with wire. I threw my hands up in the air.

"Easy, boys — I'm going with you," I said.

Still they grabbed and attempted to hustle me, but still their actions lacked intention. The door was opened and I looked in.

"You've got to be kidding me," I said.

The room was painted a pale yellow and contained nothing but a gurney with four leather straps hanging off its sides. In a corner of the ceiling, a video camera surveyed the scene. The guards hustled me in, and the door closed behind with a clang. The room was obviously designed with intimidation in mind. I could not believe they allowed this place to exist in the hospital.

I sat on the bed and looked up at the camera, which stared back unblinking. I could feel the people through the lens. I sat on the edge of the bed and gave the camera a wave.

"You think I'm afraid of this? Watch — "

I took one of the leather cuffs and strapped it around my wrist. I clipped it a little tight and went to loosen it but found that the clasp was secured by a small lock.

Oh well, I thought. I raised the cuff up to the camera and pointed to it and shrugged. With nothing much else to do, I sat there on the bed and contemplated the atrociousness of the paint job.

Within in a few minutes, the lock on the door rattled and the door opened. The two guards walked into the room, studiously talking to each other about baseball. I re-examined my impression of their gorilla-like appearance, thinking that perhaps I had been a little kind. The brawler examined the cuff I had electively placed myself in.

"I seemed to have placed the cuff on a little tight," I said. "Perhaps you could take it off now."

"If you're stupid enough to put 'em on you're going to stay in 'em," he said, flicking his gaze upon me, though his eyes barely seemed to understand what he was saying.

The guards resumed their discussion, again avoiding my eyes. Then, without warning one of them made a move for one of my legs, hanging over the side of the bed.

"Easy, son, I see ..." I said. "Let me help you." I swung my legs onto the bed.

During all this, a petite nurse walked into the room. She was dark skinned and at least over fifty. She did not wear scrubs. Instead she wore a black blouse covered with a rose print, and she carried a needle.

As she walked into the squalid room, she looked at me in such an apologetic way that I found it difficult to begrudge her.

"Don't forget my other arm," I said, and placed it in the other cuff. Still the guards avoided my eyes. To my mind, this betrayed a deep cowardice. This impression was reinforced by the fact that they began talking about baseball as though I was not even in the room. I had had enough, and it was time to strike.

"I see how this is going to go," I said. "Is this the way you do your job? Is this the way you look after people in the hospital?" Still the guards ignored me.

"You!" I said, my voice cracking around the room. The grey-haired guard who'd adjusted the cuff around my ankle looked up at me, for the first time.

"You should be ashamed of yourself."

My words ballooned around the room, enveloping the guard, and I saw my words strike home. They had a curious and profound effect. It was as though they connected with some node in the guard's brain and activated a truth he could not deny. I looked into his eyes and saw that he knew he was acting poorly and that once that truth had been activated, his mind did not know what to do with it. It consumed him, and I watched him, deflated, cast down his eyes. He looked like a little boy slapped by his mother.

I felt a pulse run through me. I had always known the power of words, but this affirmation was something new.

There was silence for a moment in the room, yet my anger still seethed.

The guard with the shaved head was the first to break the silence. Needing to recover some sense of order, perhaps, he began to mumble something about baseball.

I had been waiting for this, and I turned my attention to him.

"And you."

He said nothing, did not bring up his gaze.

"Look at me," I growled. He slowly raised his eyes.

"You should be — especially — ashamed of yourself."

I watched as that universal truth node was again activated, watched my words ricochet around the guard's skull, and again watched the somehow physical transformation from man to child.

I had to smile. At the foot of my bed stood two quivering children with downcast eyes.

The nurse slipped the needle painlessly into my leg.

"You know," I said, "in two hours, I'm just going to be awake again. Dumb motherfuckers."

I lay back, took two deep breaths, and blacked out. My last awareness was of contentment at the shame imprinted on their minds.

* * *

I opened my eyes, and through a thick haze, a lovely face appeared above me. Golden hair and blue eyes peered with a mixture of concern and kindness.

"An angel ..." I said.   I felt like I was tied down by a thousand tiny lines manned by the tiny soldiers from *Gulliver's Travels*. I tried to move, tried to think, but was pulled back.

Heather ran her hands through my hair.

"You have to get out of this place ..." she said.

Heather, yes. How did she get here — how did she know I was here?

"I called the hospital after I had not heard from you in a few days," she said, as if reading the thoughts in my mind. Or had I spoken the words?

Again I tried to move, to form a sentence. I saw anxiety in Heather's eyes. I needed to get this drug out of my system, and the only way to do that was to sleep. I squeezed her hand, gave her one of my warmest smiles, and let darkness slide back over me.

* * *

I awoke and sat up on the bed. I was back in the main room of the unit. I felt groggy but otherwise fine. A nurse came and offered me some water in a large Styrofoam cup. Not very eco-friendly, I thought, and wondered at the nature of my first fully conscious thought.

"Dr. Cerna will see you in a couple of hours," said the nurse. "Take it easy till then."

I watched her recede into the nurses' station. It was absurd — it was as though the events of just a few hours ago had never occurred. In due course, a nurse came and led me to one of the locked interview rooms, where a man waited for me.

I sat across from the doctor, who wore his receding hair shortly cropped and a checked bow tie. I had a hard and fast rule, a rule that had yet to be proven wrong, not to trust anyone who wore a bow tie — unless it was worn with a tuxedo, of course, in which case it was a whole new ball game. While I contemplated this, the doctor moved his arm to retrieve a file from his case on the table. His shirt cuffs flopped open. He wore his French-cuffed shirt with no cuff links, like a half-dressed clown. I slid my head back an inch and wondered if the bow tie and the lack of cuff links served to cancel each other out.

"Well, Philip, what do you think?" said the doctor.

"What do you mean, 'What do I think?'"

"Why do you think you're here?"

"Well, I'm here because my uncle tried to take a swing at me, called the cops, fed them some line about me being sick, and here I am."

"I see," said the doctor.

"Well, at least you see," I said.

"Your uncle tried to take a swing at you?"

"What was I supposed to do? I defended myself."

"You have a right to defend yourself."

"Exactly. Then my uncle calls the cops — he knows how the system works — and they come galloping out because, I suppose, they needed something to do. I tried to explain the situation. They weren't interested in hearing it. Then they brought me here." Silence fell between us. I wanted to broach the subject of the incident with the security guards, but Heather's words rang in my mind. I could tell the doctor was waiting for me to say something on the subject. Was he trapping me, waiting for me to lose my cool? I sat very still for a moment. Then I moved a pawn: I said nothing.

"What was the thrust of the disagreement with your uncle?" the doctor said.

"He thought I was ill."

"What do *you* think?"

"I think there is nothing wrong with me."

"I see," said Dr. Cerna.

What's with doctors always saying "I see"? I thought.

"You're here now, Philip," he said. "What would you like to do?"

I considered for a moment. "I have no place to go. I certainly can't go back to my uncle's. I've been staying on my land-locked boat, but that isn't the most comfortable of places. Do you suggest I stay here? But that would mean I'm ill, and even though everyone insists on telling me different, I don't think there is anything wrong with me. I think I really just need some space from this situation."

"It's up to you, Philip. Based on everything I've read in your file, I have my own opinion, but all that really matters is what you think." I nodded and the doctor continued. "What I can provide is place for you to consider what is happening with you. I can make some calls, have you transferred to another hospital in the city. Rivervalley Hospital is connected to some large parklands. It will give you the opportunity to go for some long walks. There are conditions, though. First, you cannot leave, as I have seen from your file you have decided to do in the past. You may walk the grounds, and the parks, but you must return to the hospital. You will find that these areas are ample and will provide you with all the space you require. Second, you must take all medication prescribed to you. It will be nothing you have not taken before, and you will discuss it with your doctor there, but it is a hospital, not a spa. What do you say?"

I considered it. "Why are you doing this for me?" I said.

"Why? Because you are a smart guy, and you are not, evidently, going to have anyone tell you that you need help. You need to come to that conclusion yourself. What I can provide is the best atmosphere for you to do this. It is the best place in this city, even this country, as far as I am concerned. What say you?"

"Frankly," I said, "I am not crazy about the last condition, but like I said, I need some space from this situation, and what you offer seems to fit the bill."

"Well?"

"I'll agree to your conditions," I said, with a curt nod of the head.

"Excellent. I'll arrange for transport in the morning. You'll stay in this unit tonight," said the doctor, rising from the table. "Also, I should apologize for the conditions you'll be staying in tonight."

"I should think you would," I said.

The doctor shot me a half smile and stuck out his hand. "All the best to you, Philip."

"Thank you, doctor," I said shaking his hand.

I followed the doctor out the door, and as the wind from the closing door thudded against my back, a small part of me was pleased.

[CHAPTER TEN]

The light of the fire is the sun, and you will not misapprehend me
if you interpret the journey upwards to be the ascent of the soul.

— Plato, *The Cave*

The next morning, at nine on the dot, two ambulance
attendants buzzed through the unit door, pushing a gurney. I
was perched on one of the vinyl beds awaiting their arrival. I
had slept only in snatches — the condition of the unit and the
proximity to other patients had made it difficult to relax.

"A gurney?" I said, as the attendant rolled it up in front of
me.

"It's regulation," said an attendant, snapping the gurney
into sitting position.

I shrugged and got on.

"Straps?" I said as one attendant buckled my torso and
legs.

"Regulations. Just try and enjoy the ride."

I wrinkled up the corners of my mouth, but decided to take
his advice. They wheeled me out the door, down the hallway,
and out to the transport ambulance.

I began to rather enjoy myself as they drove me the half
hour uptown to the new hospital. It's not often you get driven
around lying in a bed, I thought, looking out the back window

as the city went by. But like the shoot of a newly planted seed, a thought grew inside me: I began wondering why I was enjoying myself so much.

When we reached the hospital, the attendant took me up in an elevator to the ward. A plump blonde nurse greeted us at the ward entrance.

"Good morning, Philip," she said, linking her words in a southern drawl as the attendants unbuckled me from the gurney. "I'm Chrissy."

"Good morning," I said, looking around.

We were in an anteroom with three exits: a closed door leading to a well-lit hallway, the elevator we had just come up in, and a second door, with a wired glass window showing only darkness beyond. An entire wall was taken up by a long desk manned by a nurse. I was pleased to note there was no glass. I'm not sure why I was so pleased, but perhaps it had something to do with the lack of barrier between staff and patient. The open concept seemed to say, "We are here to help you — we don't need to be removed from you."

"This way, Philip," said Chrissy, gesturing to the darkened door.

I eyed her with suspicion but followed her through. The door locked behind me. To my left was a glassed-in space, beyond that, an area with metal benches bolted to the floor and a television encased in steel. A jail. Just like the one I had left. The only difference was the six doors on one side of the square that made up the room. Through these doors, I could make out six hospital beds.

"What's this?" I said, looking at the three video cameras unapologetically bolted to the ceiling.

"This is the observation room," Chrissy said lightly.

"The observation room?" I said. What was that saying ...? *A southerner will fuck you with a smile.*

"I was told I was going to a better place than the place I just left," I said. "A place where I could go for walks, get some space. I don't know what this is —" I gestured around the room, "— but it certainly isn't better."

"Philip," said Chrissy with a little pout, "it is only temporary. It is our policy here that every person has to remain in observation for twenty-four hours before they can be admitted to the ward. It's not a long time. You'll see the doctor tomorrow afternoon. We'll have you set up in your room before that. Now, I'm going to get you some lunch."

"Policy," said Philip. "That covers a multitude of evils."

"Very funny, Philip," she said.

With that she left me standing in the middle of the observation room. People seemed to be fond of leaving me standing in the middle of the room lately.

On the metal benches sat two people. One was a man with long greasy hair and an overgrown beard who played with his long fingernails, trying to dig the dirt out from beneath them. The other, a small, dark-skinned woman, sat rail straight and avoided my gaze.

I selected a room that appeared not to be in use. I sat at the foot of the bed in that narrow room, trying not to associate it with the images of a tomb that flitted into my mind. I looked up at the video camera trained on the bed.

Great, I thought, and flipped the camera the bird.

* * *

The next morning Chrissy came and collected me from the observation room. Together we walked through the locked door, into the anteroom, past the nurses' station, and through the only remaining door. It was like walking through an airlock. The hallway was painted a light green, the walls covered with patients' art projects and lovely prints.

The hallway was long and had two dozen doors running off it.

"This is one of our lounges," said Chrissy gesturing to her left. The room was surrounded in low shelves stuffed with puzzles, magazines, toys, and art supplies. There was a large television with a semicircle of comfortable armchairs.

"To your right is the laundry room," she said as we continued down the hallway. "The three washers and dryers are for your use. Also all the fresh bedding and towels are stored here and you can get them as you need them."

"The men's shower and restroom," said Chrissy, knocking on a door and opening it.

The bathroom gleamed white. I stepped into the room. The three shower stalls and sinks were spotless.

"Not bad," I said as we continued down the hall.

"This will be your room," said Chrissy.

The room contained two hospital beds, neither in use, and a cupboard and nightstands with lamps.

"You'll have your own room for now," said Chrissy. "Last, I'll show you the main lounge and eating area."

We pasted a buzzing ice machine as we approached the room at the end of the hall. When we stepped through the doorway, the sun blazed through the windows, hitting me full in the face. Three sides of the room sported floor-to-ceiling windows that overlooked a small ravine.

The majority of the room was taken up by a long table, around which a dozen people sat eating lunch. "The main lounge," said Chrissy. "Also there is a phone for your use. Have some lunch and then you'll meet with the doctor." She said passed me a tray of food from a wheeled rack.

The people sitting around the table seemed happy enough. Some wore hospital gowns, some chatted to their neighbours, some silently ate their meals. A few people looked up and smiled as I came and sat down at the end of the table. I ate my meal wordlessly. The food was made palatable only by the addition of large quantities of salt and pepper from the gaggle of white packets strewn about the table. Three middle-aged woman sat around a corner of the table giggling and occasionally looking up at me, smiling. They got up in unison and left the room to return a few moments later, their lips painted and their cheeks powdered with too much rouge. It was flattering, in a way, despite the fact that they all now looked like prostitutes past their prime.

"Time to meet the doctor, Philip," said Chrissy after I had finished my meal.

We walked down the hall to a small meeting room with a round table. Presently the doctor came in. He was of average height and had an Eastern European look about him. He wore a starched white shirt tucked into jeans and snappy brown shoes. Though I tried, I could not object to his appearance.

The doctor sat a quarter circle away from me, put a file to one side, and extended his hand.

"I'm Dr. Wilinski. I run this ward. Pleasure."

"Pleasure," I said, taking the proffered hand.

"I've spoken to Dr. Cerna, of course, but just so you know, he's relayed the substance of your conversation the other day. Let's be clear. You've expressed a desire for quiet. A place to remove yourself from the occurrences that have seemed to be piling up around you. Also, some family and other doctors have informed you that you could be suffering from an active phase of a bipolar condition, hypomania or mania. But, as I understand, you are not convinced of the diagnosis."

"So far so good," I said, rather liking this direct approach.

"Have you been diagnosed with this before?"

"Yes," I said. "I thought you would be aware of that."

Dr. Wilinski shrugged a shoulder.

"Maybe five or six years ago I was first diagnosed," I added.

"Have you taken medication for this?" asked the doctor.

"Yes, on and off, but as you said, I'm not convinced of the diagnosis, so it makes it difficult to decide to keep taking the medicine."

"Do you have a doctor who monitors your medication?"

"I see Dr. Sheffield. I've seen her for many years. She's actually based at the hospital I just came from," I said.

"Dr. Sheffield, yes, I know her well — in fact, I trained her."

"That's very interesting," I said. Dr. Sheffield was the finest doctor I had ever met. That Dr. Wilinski had trained her spoke volumes about him.

"Dr. Cerna has also told me," he continued, "that you've agreed to the conditions of staying in this unit. You'll have access to the parklands. You're free to walk around the hospital grounds, grab a coffee, but you must take only short leaves from the ward. We can't help you if you're not around. Agreed?"

"Agreed," I said.

"Now I know you have some questions about your diagnosis, and I appreciate that. But I'm going to be straight with you. From everything I've seen, you have a textbook active case of hypomania, maybe even mania. And I mean textbook. If I open up any textbook on the subject and read the symptoms, nine out of ten apply to you. The good news is this makes my job very easy. So in accordance with the second condition of your stay, I want you to take the medication I prescribe."

"At least no one can accuse you of being uncandid," I said. "I'm here to resolve this situation, and it sounds like I'll have plenty of time to consider what you say."

I sat back and took a breath. I watched as a bolt of irritation flashed through me. Upon its passing, I wondered where it came from. A lot of what the doctor was saying made sense. Why the resistance?

"Very well," he said, "I'm going to prescribe valproic acid and Zyprexa."

"Hold on," I said, bridling. "Zyprexa is an anti-psychotic. I'm not sure I'm comfortable taking that. It's serious stuff. You're going to have to give me a better reason than your say-so. You had better explain it to me in a way that will unequivocally convince me. I don't know if anyone told you I have, let's say, a strong science background. So lay it on me."

"It is a serious medication, and it can seriously help you," began Dr. Wilinski. "Let me explain to you how it works and why I am prescribing it?"

"A good start," I said.

"We will be searching for the lowest dose of medication that can help you. As you know, there are three main neurotransmitters in the brain: dopamine, serotonin, and norepinephrine. Dopamine is the neurotransmitter responsible for focus and concentration — the same thing as effected by cocaine and, to a lesser extent, nicotine."

"Mmm," I said.

"In a mania-type situation, thoughts and emotions are large — inflamed, if you will. Concurrently, the brain is being flooded with large quantities of dopamine. These large thoughts and emotions, already taking up a big portion of one's cognitive properties, in a sense become stuck in the brain because of the high levels of dopamine. Like I said, the dopamine is responsible for focus. The brain focuses on, or latches onto, these thoughts, making it very difficult to let them go. Large emotions such as anger and sexuality multiply exponentially because of the high levels of dopamine. This manifests itself in many ways, such as unsafe sexual practices or heightened irritability. By the same principle, thoughts that are large and complex can be difficult to let go. A prime example of this is heightened religious intensity."

It sounded to me like being high on cocaine for a month, which was a pretty accurate description of how I'd felt for the last month.

"I remember walking by a church a few weeks back and being almost consumed by everything," I said, staring into the middle distance. "I spent a lot of time looking at the crosses, stained glass windows, doors. It was all so interesting, but at the same time, a part of me was vaguely disturbed. I've never had much interest in religion."

"Exactly. The iconology of religion is strongly embedded in our culture. Consequently, the thoughts associated with them are large. The dopamine helps the mind to intently examine these large thoughts. Dopamine also is responsible for making a person feel good, the reward system in the brain. You following me?"

"So far," I said, glancing out the window. It was a bright day, but unseasonably cool — hints of autumn were already on the air that pushed through the window frame, prickling my skin with goosebumps.

"Like rats in a maze," I continued. "The ones with artificially high levels of dopamine will go for the cheese over and over, regardless of whether they are hungry. They'll do this until there is no more cheese or they die."

"Very good," said Dr. Wilinski. "So you can understand that is why it feels so good, being locked in these thoughts: the more one examines, the better it feels. But this eventually becomes debilitating. What the medication does is inhibit the dopamine production and help the brain regain its equilibrium — help one unlock from thoughts."

"It seems to make sense," I said, furrowing my brow.

"It has some other effects," he continued. "It can make you quite tired. That is why we will start you on a very low dose, gradually increasing the level, searching for the lowest *functional* dose. And the medication is not forever. They are to deal with the active phase. Eventually we get rid of some, and what remains acts like a buffer preventing the active phase from recurring. Maintenance, really."

Maintenance. There was something I really liked about that. It was something basic, without complication. Something with no existential implications, something as simple as brushing your teeth.

"I read you," I said.

"Great," said the doctor, rising to leave. "I'll give the prescription order to the nurses. We'll meet every couple of days to see how you're getting on. And one last thing: Don't leave. Stay here, at the ward. You may want to leave, but don't. I think we can really help you here."

I inclined my head. The doctor turned and opened the meeting-room door.

"Doctor," I said, and Dr. Wilinski turned back to face me.

"Nice place you got here."

* * *

The days and weeks past quickly. With them evaporated my preconceived notions of what a sanatorium was like. I often thought of the great artists who had taken refuge in places like this — van Gogh, de Maupassant ... I spent my days in the groups that I was encouraged to attend. We did simple art projects, discussed nutrition and good personal habits. Many of the groups were not for me, I knew, but they gave me something to do. I was also surprised by the people in the ward. They were, for the most part, affable and quite intelligent. I often wondered if it was *because* they were intelligent, because they saw much, much more than others, that they were here for refuge. Here for a place to sort it out. Even after discussions with the doctor, I was uncertain. Still, I had a place to think it over, and that was all I wanted.

Every other day I would palm the medicine that Chrissy brought me. Once or twice she even asked to see my mouth after I swallowed water from the requisite Styrofoam cup. "Them's the deal," she'd reply to my protests as I opened my mouth and rolled the pills in my cupped hand. This, coupled with the fact that I knew I was on a very low dose of medicine — extremely low for a guy of two hundred pounds — ensured a negligible dose in practice. I didn't know why I did this, but if I'd had to guess, I'd have said it had to do with needing time to process.

In the unit, everyone seemed to get along well, with only the occasional spat, which was bound to happen with so many strangers living in such proximity.

I spent long hours walking in the parks. The weather was turning slowly from summer to fall, though the trees had not yet turned their colours. The air was warm and pleasant but the breeze cool, notes of fall detectable on its tendrils. On one occasion I walked past a church that sat next to the hospital. I spent a long time examining its gothic structure, the placement of it statues and iconology. After a time I was not even sure why I was still there. The doctor's words snuck into my head, and I wondered at their wisdom. I forcibly removed myself from the proximity of the church, feeling that all its trappings were just that — a trap.

The nurses were pleasant, though occasionally they copped an attitude, which I dispersed with a verbal shot. I met with a nurse/social worker who helped me arrange lodgings for when I decided to leave. I was sure that eventually I would patch things up with my uncle, but it would be impossible to live with him.

Gradually, I began to enjoy myself at the unit, though from time to time I was distracted by thoughts about why exactly it was I was enjoying myself. More than that, I was actually becoming highly concerned about why I was enjoying myself. As well, I still felt compelled to walk for hours.

One evening, when I'd been at the ward for over two weeks, I was walking out. I was supposed to be back at the ward shortly, and they would miss me, but I didn't care. Strong emotions were swirling within me, and I needed to think.

As dusk and then darkness fell, I followed a path through the ravine system. The branches of tall, old trees curved overhead, caverning me below. As I crested a hill, a small riding stable came into view. I stopped and looked at the stables, the barn, and the white-fenced riding ring. A light mist clung to the feet of the stables and hovered over the wet grass.

I knew the stables well. Until this moment I had forgotten they were here. When my parents had died, my uncle had enrolled me here for a summer of riding camp. I had been only twelve or thirteen. Every day I would run to the stable to brush the horses, saddle them up, and lead them to the ring. Massive, beautiful beasts they were. I'd been the only male at the camp but it hadn't mattered to me. At the end of every two-week session, we would have a competition of jumping and dressage. I did well. In fact, I often won, beating the bratty girls. I would win with a mixture of glee and sadness, for I saw the effect of my wins in the girls' tears.

I turned away from the stables and looked up at the canopy above me. I felt the breeze on my skin, saw it rustle the branches above. I inhaled deeply. What am I doing here? I thought. Why am I starting to enjoy myself? I was the best rider at that camp. I've studied in the best universities in the country. I belong in many places, but I do not belong here. What in the name of all that is holy am I doing in a mental health ward?

That memory, that thought of myself, was not so potent in its content, but in juxtaposition to my present situation, it was painful. In that tension, a seed grew within me, like the seed of a new star. I felt its untold energy, its atoms fusing.

I sat heavily on a bench under the branches; the pale yellow of a street lamp illuminated the bench and the green leaves around me. I inhaled deeply. What was the quote by Rumi? I thought. Something like "Break down the walls of the house and find stones of truth beneath them, for if you do not, the walls will break down anyway." Thinking of this, another quotation, from my meditation teacher, flashed into my mind: "See things how they actually are." Perhaps this is a good time as any to be still, I thought.

In the half-lit fog, I filled my lungs and strongly exhaled. On the next breath I did not force the air. I simply allowed the passage of air to flow through my lungs, through me. It is some time since I have done this, I thought, allowed for stillness. And no tool for stillness is closer than the breath ...

Before I had finished the thought, I noticed that my attention was no longer on my breathing. I gently returned my attention back to feeling the flow of breath ... searching, feeling the spot where the in-breath turned into the out-breath, the out-breath turned into the in-breath.

"Turn your attention to your thoughts. Watch them move like images across a screen, like clouds in the sky, patches of fog across a glen. Note the emotional weight of these thoughts: that some have little weight and others have larger weight. If you get caught in the thought, return to the breath." I silently cursed my teacher's words, realizing that I was not feeling my breath — instead, I was focusing on these words.

I returned to my breath, but again his words, in one form or another, inserted themselves into my mind.

I've never understood that anyway, I thought, and gently returned to my breath, feeling it enter my body, nourishing me. One, two, three consecutive breaths, then the thought came: Let's try it — follow the instructions.

I returned once more, connecting on the in-breath, feeling the moisture-rich air enter my body.

My foot is itchy, came a thought, and I thought of my foot. I noticed this and returned to my breath.

My uncle is a prick ... I thought of my uncle. I noticed my mind on my uncle, and, with considerable effort, I returned to my breath.

Dr. Wilinksi is not a bad guy ... It's a nice evening ... The trees are lovely ... But somehow these thoughts were different: I saw them move across my mind as images on a screen, and none had much emotional draw.

"It's a pleasant evening" moved across my consciousness, emerging from blackness and disappearing again into blackness. I felt as though I were standing in a dark cave behind a surging waterfall whose crashing waters were a deep blue, streaked white in places by the velocity of the water.

"My uncle's a prick" came into my consciousness over the edge of the waterfall, and somehow it was held statically in the rushing indigo water. I noticed the massive emotional content of this thought. I felt its draw, as though the sheer volume of surging water was pulling me into the falls. Just before the water, the torrent of thought, took me, I felt as if I could actually look about the cave. The cave was carved into black and grey rock, and its roughly hewn walls were barely illuminated by the light that emanated from the falls — a bluish illumination, as though the water had some form of phosphorescence. Dark green mosses flecked the rocks; a grey, gritty sand covered the floor.

I braced my feet against that sandy floor. It was no use. The draw of the falls, the draw of the thought, began to pull me. I began to skid toward the falls, my feet leaving deep gouges in the grey sand. I looked again at the falls. They were, without question, beautiful, their power unmistakable.

I did not fear the draw of the water, but I was aware of a desire, a want, to not enter the stream. I began to struggle, pressing my feet harder into the sand, but still I was pulled. The gouges in the grey sand deepened around my heels. I could not deny the draw of the water, and I all but resigned myself to it. Resigned all but the desire to not enter the stream. Even at the precipice that desire did not diminish.

Breathe!

I felt breath turn from in-breath to out-breath, and in that feeling, in that place, in that shift of attention, I was released.

I was standing in the middle of the cave watching the waterfall. The thought that had been held there in the surging torrent of water, images of my uncle linked with pain and anger, was held there for a moment longer, and then, as though its mooring clamps were unlocked, it was swept down the falls and evaporated into the blackness of my consciousness, evaporated from my vision like mist on a cold night.

———

He saw thoughts streaming through his mind, moving like clouds in the sky. It was a state of pure observation. The thoughts came at random, and they came as he willed. He could see them as large billowing thunderclouds or as tufts as on a hot summer day. It all depended on the emotional content, the weight that they held. Often he could see these thoughts as disproportionate to reality.

What is reality?

He saw that enormous cloud and let it pass out of his consciousness.

The thoughts were disproportionate to reality — too much anger, too much pain. A type of unbalance was there. The thought did not particularly bother him much. The mind can often become imbalanced. Too much coffee, dehydration — the solution: drink water. A fever: Tylenol, to break the hallucination. Too little sleep, irritability: catch some sleep. For him, the imbalance was nothing more than that, and it required simple attention — a type of Tylenol, a type of medicine, like water for dehydration.

But there was more.

There was a small inkling of something below this triteness. Perhaps it was what had driven him to this point ... What had caused this? He knew not and cared not, but if he had to guess, it was a type of intelligence, the ability to see deeply into things. Perhaps it was more like a gift — a gift whose power he had not learned to harness, like a racing yacht in a gale.

In a way, what others called "illness" he now saw as a gift. It had given him the opportunity to see the internal workings of the mind. He thought back to that first meditation class, the lesson wrapped in pain and anguish but burning like the light of a newly formed star: We are not our thoughts, we are not our emotions. He had seen his mind inflamed ... He had seen his mind squeezed between the boulders of ill thought. He realized that when the mind was harmonized, as balanced as a Buddha on a mountainside, one could still step outside thought, outside emotion, and evaluate their validity.

In this way, one could operate the mind like a gearshift in a car, like a jet's ailerons. One could look closely at the workings of the mind. One could choose whether to believe their emotions, their thoughts, or one could not. And one could choose how to respond.

Choice.

What are we? he asked himself. He supposed he understood now that we are that spark, that thing that separates the animate from the inanimate — the dragonfly from the stone. The thing that contains thought and emotion.

We are not our thoughts, we are not our emotions. That was the gift. And maybe, just maybe, the heat, what others called "illness," was the burning of a useless husk of consciousness as the soul flew upward to a greater awareness.

As the soul moved toward an awareness of itself, the burning of awakening was felt. This awakening was the soul's upward journey to the light of awareness; for it is hot there, as hot as standing on the ocean of the sun. As touching the raw wire of life.

———

I snapped my eyes open. I saw the mist of the night, hazily illuminated in the pale yellow of the street lamp, eddying around me, swirling into the foliage above my head, and eviscerating itself on the green leaves.

There it was, all laid out before me: The emotions, huge. The ability to see them. The gift of understanding, gleamed through the flames of illness. The ability to see the world through two lenses, not one: the true realms of existence and the established realities. The matrix of understanding that flows from this understanding. Yes. It was a bit like that movie,

The Matrix. The world was full of mysteries, but to exist on the fringe, in the fusion of the mysteries, would burn me up. It was better, was it not, to enter these places at any time and then to come back and play in the matrix of established reality, lest my wings melt and I plummet to the earth? To exist in the mysteries, yes — but not at the price of my mortal coils.

I could see that a simple, small part of this was medicine. It would allow my thoughts to become manageable, not unlike a guard against crushing, cold depression. For I saw now: what goes up must come down. The price of dwelling in the hot heart of mystery was an equal amount of time spent in the glacier of depression. But I could go in and out, *maintain* this equilibrium. It *was* like maintenance, nothing more, nothing less — a tool, which would assist me in turn to wield my mind. "Be the change you want to see in the world," Gandhi had said. Who was to say how this equanimity of peace would be carried forward into the world around me? But it must, for we are all connected, and any other thought on the subject is but an illusion.

I knew not where these thoughts came from. It was as though I stood in a cool river and these thoughts flowed around me, through me.

I had awoken.

And there it was, the gift. I saw clearly the workings of my own mind, how the mind works. I had some space around thought, around emotion. I had space around my situation, and I could choose. I knew it to be true that the emotion I experienced when I thought of my uncle was disproportionate to the truth. Was he not simply trying to do his best? If I were in the same position, would I not do the same? Maybe, maybe not. He had been wrong on many scores, but could you fault a man for doing everything in his power to help the child he had raised? And if my thought could be disproportionate around such a large issue, could it not also be so for other things?

I rose from the bench and made for the hospital through the greenery. I tried the experience again, this time focusing on the impact of my feet, the feeling in my body.

Thump, thump, thump.

The sound of my own feet striking the moist asphalt, reverberating through my body. As a thought came into my mind, I watched it flow by. Sometimes I would get caught up in thinking these thoughts that wandered into my mind, whatever they would be. Thoughts of family, thoughts of the weather, old memories.

When I noticed this, I began the process again, breathing deeply, feeling the fall of my feet on the ground.

Thump, thump, thump. And I watched as the thoughts receded into blackness.

As I neared the hospital, emerging from the dark ravine onto the periphery of the well-lit grounds, something had stuck with me. The majority of my thoughts around my situation had strong emotion attached to them. That emotion was often disproportionate to what really was happening.

Thump, thump, thump.

It was not my way, I reflected, to be reactive, to press upon the boundaries of violence. I am a calm and even-headed person, I thought. I recalled all the sailing I had done, something that only could be done with equanimity. Now I was easily distracted, on a hair trigger, getting caught in situations that I should have seen coming as far as the horizon. I thought of my martial training — aikido, the art of peace, something that can be learned only through magnanimity; for though a powerful self-defence skill, it is also, at its core, used to teach another his or her errors, and by such emanate and cultivate peace to the web of humanity around oneself.

I stopped in front of the sprawling hospital campus, pebbles grinding under my feet. It shimmered in the darkness. I could see that the only reason I was here was because I would not have anyone else tell me I was ill — it was something I had to conclude myself. I realized that I had been watching myself all this long while, watching my own mind. I realized that I was given no choice, that my thoughts my emotions were too big, and I wanted them back ...

I breathed sharply three times, hearing the oxygen rasping through my lungs. Here I am, I said to myself.

* * *

I swung up the stairs to the unit, where, when I opened the heavy door, Chrissy was waiting for me.

"Where have you been, Philip?" she said. I silenced her with a levelled gaze.

"I need to speak to the doctor, right now," I said. "I'll be in my room." I turned my back on her and walked down the hall.

After a few steps, I turned back. "Oh yes," I said. "Do you have my evening medicine?"

"Yes, of course. I'll bring it to your room." she said, puzzlement on her face. I looked at her and a realization struck me. She was asleep. Not in the literal sense — it was something more ethereal than that, something finer. She was not exactly present in the present. It was a thought that I had been carrying for a long time about a lot of people — in fact, the majority of people I met — but a thought that had lingered just under my consciousness, awaiting recognition. I liked that: *re-cognition. Re-thinking:* something always known but forgotten.

"Thank you, ma'am," I said, imitating her southern lilt.

Dr. Wilinski knocked on my door and stepped in. I stood leaning against the wall with my arms and legs crossed.

"You're lucky you caught me, Philip. I was just packing up for the day. What's the big emergency?"

"I'm done playing. I just wanted you to know that."

The doctor said nothing but made a small motion with his right eyebrow. I could tell that he wanted some explanation, something to justify this change in attitude, but I was not ready to discuss my experience. I simply gazed at him in silence.

"Very well," he said, "but why?"

"I don't belong here," I replied.

The doctor looked down and appeared to be thinking it all over.

"That sounds a little ... vain, Philip," he said, a small challenge poking through his tone. Prickling.

"Phssah ..." The sound of air pushing through my nostrils was my only response. I felt anger at his words pulse through me, but instead of acting, I breathed. I acknowledged the anger to myself. Held it in my mind, and marvelled at how it floated away.

Was it worth explaining it all to him? I looked at him, at his entire aspect. It was different from Chrissy's. Yes, he would understand: he was awake, my brain told me. Yet I remained guarded. My uncle had always told me that actions speak louder than words. So I bided my time. Did others know of the true nature of the mind?

The doctor looked at me still. Wanting something more. I chose my words carefully. "I've heard vanity runs through all things. It runs through the Diplomat's negotiations, through the Thief's plundering, through the Lover's attention," I said.

I said this not so much to throw him off the scent, nor because it contained some elements of truth, the depth of which could only be recognized to those who had some understanding of the nature of emotion, nor to test him, though my words certainly contained elements of all of these. Mostly I said it because I had read it somewhere and had always wanted to say it. And because it seemed so perfect.

I could see the corners of his eyes crinkle in a smile. Just then Chrissy entered with a little paper cup of pills.

So that was it — simple in the end, really. The medicine was a tool, a small part of the whole. Useful for my body, like salt or vitamins, to maintain balance. Perhaps I could do without it. Perhaps I could go on my boat and meditate for a month, but why bother? Why risk the blood-boiling highs, the glacial lows? I could use the medicine like a guard, a buffer against these dangers, and use the gift to achieve ... whatever the fuck I wanted. I thought all this in a moment, and more, much more.

"Thanks, Chrissy," I said. Celebration Warrior Maintenance, I said to myself, like a mantra.

Celebration: To heal to be alive, one could kiss the feet of the inventors of this medicine. To have learned what I learned; for I knew that the medicine was nothing — nothing — without awareness.

Warrior: I had battled the enemy of my own mind, and I could not think of a fiercer opponent. For that is what I was and that was what my mind would become — a warrior, a sword.

Maintenance: To wield the mind, one must maintain it. We all have to do this, with sleep, attending to our issues, feeding the body. The ancient tenet of *Budō*, the samurai code, says, "Of the sword: one must not neglect maintenance." If my mind was to be a sword, it must be maintained, sharpened, polished, cared for like the blade always carried by the samurai in every waking and sleeping moment. For the samurai, the sword was an extension of the soul, and thus the mind.

I knocked back the pills.

"Hey, Doc, have your heard this one?" I said. "I used to think the mind was the most important part of the body until I realized what was telling me that."

"Actually, Philip, I have heard that one," he said, and I could not be sure, but I thought I heard joy dripping from his words.

"It might be a good idea to up my medicine to a level more suited to my weight, maybe even higher. At least for a short time, I will take responsibility for the side effect. I can handle it."

"Okay, Philip, I'll order up those changes, and I take it you'll no longer be moderating your own dosages?"

And so, with this matrix of understanding, began the sharpening of my mind, like a katana, that ancient samurai weapon, the edge meditatively sharp, holding the mysteries of the Divine.

* * *

The higher dose was a little difficult to handle. I was tired for large parts of the day, and I slept long hours. But I coupled this with long meditative walks, no longer driven and staring and being trapped but feeling my body as I walked. I used the exercise and the techniques of meditation to empty my mind, not unlike a clogged drain.

I would sit on a bench each day in the cooling air and meditate, feeling my breath — and that was all. In the beginning, I was lucky to get five minutes out of my efforts before I would jump up, spitting in frustration. But gradually my focus extended, first ten minutes, then fifteen, till I could sit for a half hour without difficulty.

Along with my focus returned my desire to write. I would scribble lines of poems onto whatever paper I could scrounge. It was therapeutic to allow my emotions and thoughts to flow onto the page unvetted.

I requested a razor from the staff, which, surprisingly, seemed to be as difficult as signing out an M16 from the military. What do you want it for? Where will you keep it? How often will you use it? Well, I want it to ... shave, I replied. I will keep it in my drawer. I will uses it every few days or as needed.

On one of my walks, I slipped out down the road to a barber and had him do something with the mop on my head. It seemed to work, for when I returned, the nurse manning the door said, "Is there something I can do for you, sir?"

With only a few days left in my stay, there was one thing I had to do. I sat by the window in my room looking at the patch of manicured grass outside my window. If they gave me that patch of earth to garden, I could be just like van Gogh, I chuckled to myself. Arrogance knows no bounds.

Down the hall, I sidled up to the telephone. It was a little after nine in the morning. I dialled a number.

"Good morning — Hyde & Associates," came the voice of Elizabeth, my uncle's receptionist.

"Hi, Elizabeth," I said, dispensing with formality. "Could I speak to my uncle?"

"Hello, Philip," she said, her voice all warmth now. "You could if you were in Stockholm."

"Stockholm, Sweden?" I said.

"Yes, he left to visit some family — just up and left last week, said he needed a break. He didn't tell you?"

"No one ever tells me anything," I said.

"He is like that sometimes," she laughed.

"Too true," I said. "Have a good one, Elizabeth."

I hung up the phone and sat looking at it. I again lifted the receiver. It felt greasy against my ear, and I rubbed it on my jeans before I dialled again. After no more than two rings, my uncle's voice crackled over the phone.

"Stockholm, eh?" I said.

"... Hello, Philip," he said. It was amazing how in two words I could hear his attention ramped up to max. "How are you?"

"Good, I'm good," I said.

"So I hear," he said. I had to laugh — he always had his sources.

"Uncle?"

"Yes," he said.

"I forgive you," I said. I heard relief in his exhale. I hung up the phone without waiting for any other response.

I walked slowly down the hall, staring at the floor, hands shoved deeply in my pockets.

* * *

A week and a half later, I was in my room packing my bag. I felt calmer, focused. None of the wild uncontrolled driving focus that compelled me to walk for hours to examine iconology. No shortness of temper. This had been replaced by the soft, powerful focus that I knew I had, a shimmering focus that was beautiful to look at. A knock announced Dr. Wilinski.

"Last day, Philip."

"That's right," I said, placing my final shirt into my bag and zipping it up.

"I wanted to say my goodbyes. Why don't I walk you out?" he said. I pulled on my blazer and grabbed my bag. Together we walked down the hall.

"I just want you to know you've been an exemplary patient," he said. "It's remarkable how quickly you have healed."

"Thank you, Doctor. You and I both know it's not just the medicine that is responsible," I said, as we reached the exit.

"Indeed," he said, and extended his hand. I shook it with warmth, for I felt his compliment was one of the deepest that he had at his disposal. The difficulties I had endured flashed through my mind. What was my reward for all my troubles? An understanding of the nature of the world, the mind — that's all.

"Oh yes," I said. "Doctor, I have something for you." From my breast pocket I extracted a piece of paper, precisely folded in half.

"When I first came here," I said, "I noted all the art you had on the wall. It put me at ease."

"Well, we do the best with what we have," he replied. He opened the paper and read, his face tight with concentration.

"It's a poem," I said as he read it. "Perhaps you may want to put it up, my small contribution." I turned and walked away, fancying that the doctor watched me go, an enigmatic expression writ on his face.

At the bottom of the stairs, I paused at the doorway. I pushed it open and the sun smashed through. The day was a shade warmer than cool; the breeze that filtered in through the doorway vacillated between cool and warm. I filled my lungs with the green-scented air that rolled off the parklands and stepped through the doorway. The date was September 21, my birthday.

Through a forest dark
    I walked
surrounded
        on three sides by a
she-Wolf
an emancipated Tiger
a lurking Lion
        Knowing fear
I fought with light of knowledge
As I stepped into the light
        blades bloodied
pockets bulging with jewels
I wanted
to name
        it
to give it form, shape
and it
resisted my naming.
It
        existed
                beyond
                        name
As I looked at the
stoic pines with so much
to share
I wanted to believe that
it was greater than the sum of its parts
more
than its name
        And I do.

— Philip Hyde

Acknowledgements:

Let me tell you a little story. I sat on my front stoop with my father, and explained: Why writing. I told him, as JFK said, "We do it, not because it is easy, but because it is hard." In future, I will have to be more careful wielding my quotes. In the years that followed that conversation, I often reflected on how much work it must have been to go to the moon. This, as I became cognizant of how much work it takes to write a book.

Thanks to my dad and my mom. My dad for his unflinching, rock-like support. Without my mom's tether to *this* earth, well, I'd probably be bitting my own neck.

Thanks to Stephanie Fysh, my editor.

Dr. M - my doctor, my friend, my counsel. Brilliant.

Thanks to all my friends.

Thanks to all who read, and edited early versions of the manuscript and told me, more!

Thanks to my love.

And thanks to you.

JAWALDIN.COM

Like the book? Please leave a review at your favourite online retailer.